HIGH SEAS & HIGH STAKES

Books: 1-2

TAMARA GILL

HIS LADY SMUGGLER

HIGH SEAS & HIGH STAKES, BOOK 1

After two failed seasons in town, May Stanford sees her future no longer with her family, but in a nearby convent where she'll not be anyone's financial burden. But before she can embark on her new life, May must complete her dealings with the local smugglers, men who have kept a roof over her family's head during frugal times. One last Christmas at home and her life would change forever. So when

William Scott, the Earl of Grandison arrives and crumbles her perfectly planned future to rubble, May is less than pleased.

William, Lord Grandison works for the Crown, and is determined to catch the nuisance Englishmen who dare smuggle along the Cornwall coast. William has never veered from his pursuit of these men working against the law, that was until he meets May Stanford, the maddening daughter of his host for Christmas. May drives him to distraction and forces him to admit to feelings he has never felt before.

But when May and William discover the crippling truth of each other, their secrets will threaten to tear them apart.

CHAPTER 1

Cornwall – 1811

May stared at her father, who sat nestled against the squabs of their family carriage. Thin-lipped, he perused the literature the mother superior from the Convent of the Little Sisters of Jesus had handed him just before their departure.

Granted, becoming a nun wasn't what most women longed for. A husband, children, friends and an active social life in London was what most well to do debutantes aspired to.

She no longer lived under the misapprehension such a dream would ever come to fruition for her. Firstly, they lived too many miles from the capital to travel each year for the Season, and secondly, they lacked the connections or money to fund subsequent Seasons, which, unfortunately, May required after her mortifying Coming Out.

Not to mention too many years had passed now for her to bother with all the fuss. Now at the ripe old age of four and twenty, her chances of finding a husband were slim.

And, in all truth, she no longer wanted a spouse to dictate and tell her what to do or how to live. Life this far from the capital had showed her another side of life, and it was one she'd grown to love and wouldn't give up no matter what fob bowed before her.

Her little brother sat beside her, staring in silence at the ocean to the left of the carriage. He was angry at her decision, his sullen face throwing daggers at her every so often. But she refused to be a burden to him in the years to come. It would be hard enough for her sibling to keep the estate without the added stress of a spinster sister who ate his food and needed clothing and board. Becoming a nun allowed her the life she wanted to lead without straining her family's coffers.

"Explain to me again just why a beautiful young woman such as you wishes to lock herself away in such a place. Now, don't get me wrong, May, I've always encouraged you to make your own decisions, but it's a convent. You'll be married to God. I fear you will regret your choice," her father said.

May cringed, hating his dejected tone, or that she'd had the same argument numerous times with her papa. Today, finally, she'd been able to persuade him to make the five-mile trip to the convent and meet the mother superior. It may not have been what she'd always wanted, but it was for the best considering her changed opinion on husbands and the family's circumstances, which were worsening every year. "This is my choice to make. I know it's not something you agree with, but I'll be happy there. I know I will." She forced herself to sit back and take a calming breath, as she tried to enjoy the view of the Cornwall coast as much as she could.

He raised a suspicious eyebrow. "Which of us are you

trying to persuade? I think it's a mistake." He paused. "You are allowed to change your mind, my dear. You only have to say so."

"It is done now and there is nothing left to discuss. I have only a few weeks before I must return, so please," she said, her voice sounding unsteady even to her own ears, "let's make my last few weeks and this Christmas the best we've ever had. I want us to enjoy ourselves, be happy. Please try and accept my choice."

Her father huffed out a breath and stared at the ocean. The silence threatened to consume her, along with a flutter of panic over the fact the rest of her life would be full of prayer and religion. But if it allowed her independence and freedom of will, then it was a small toll to pay.

Even though they were not an overly religious family, the thought of becoming a ladies companion would never suit her, she was too outspoken for such employment, but a convent here in Cornwall, not far from home, where she could visit often, and enjoy her beloved sea suited her more than anything else.

Days of camping on the beach, swimming and enjoying the type of pastime she'd always loved would surely end, should she marry. No gentleman wanted a hellion for a wife. And yet, the mother superior had stated should she attend her chores and not miss prayer time, she could pursue her hobbies without censure. It was the most perfect solution to her worries. And sitting in church, praying for the good of others and taking care of the sick wasn't something she would shy away from. If anything she looked forward to the quiet, and keeping herself company.

May smiled. She was doing the right thing and that knowledge outweighed the youthful desire to marry for love and have children of her own. Those dreams had dried up along with any offers of marriage. Not that she received any...

Of course had the family had an abundance of funds, May could've tried for a third season, but it wasn't to be. It had taken some years to stomach the thought of becoming an old-maid or nun, but it no longer bothered her and she was now content with her choice.

She looked across at her little brother, ten years her junior and calm washed over her like a wave. She loved him more than anything, and it was no sacrifice to ensure his future flowed with ease of purpose, and with her tucked away at a convent not being a drain on his funds, that's exactly how he'd live. But oh, how she would miss her brother's informative and always enthusiastic conversations about science or history. Never did they have boring or stilted conversations at dinner.

The carriage turned into their family's cliff-top drive and May thought she caught a glimpse of a ship. Sitting back against the squabs, she wondered if Stephen, Captain Doherty had come early... Surely not, he wasn't due for some weeks, well after New Year's.

"Matthew, you have studies to attend to when we return. As for you, May, I'll see you at dinner."

She nodded, but didn't reply to the curt dismissal or react to his glower. It was obvious her father would take some time to come to terms with her decision. Her family were angry and upset, but hopefully, they would come around to her way of thinking eventually.

The carriage pulled up before their home. May stepped out first and turned away from the front door, instead heading for the beach. Sunset was only an hour away, so she wanted to enjoy what little light she had left during these precious weeks left at home. All too soon such walks to the beach would be impossible, both by her relocation to the convent, but also the damp, chilling winds of winter would be upon them. Cornwall, the most beautiful place to live was also, one of the hardest.

May walked the well-worn track that wove its way down the steep incline to the beach. Due to the shape of the cove, it was well-protected from the elements and the water was reasonably shallow and safe for swimming during the summer months.

She sat, kicked off her boots and squished the sand between her toes. Scooping some into her palm, she opened her fingers and watched it filter through her hand, enjoying the sensation of the grains as they trickled to the ground. The ocean swept calm waves against the golden earth and drew her eye toward the horizon where she started at the sight she beheld.

A sailing ship rocked on the waves beyond the reef, its sails furled as if stationary. Were they anchored there, and if so, why were they? She squinted and from this distance could just make out a few men scurrying about on deck. But it wasn't a ship she recognized, certainly none of the smuggling vessels she was familiar with. Her friend and smuggling partner Stephen, wasn't due to shore for some weeks yet. So who was out there?

She stood and shaded her eyes to get a better view and stilled when she noticed a small wooden craft headed for shore. She'd not noticed it hidden in the waves while she sat. A lone passenger rowed the boat with ease and great precision toward her beach.

With her gaze fixed firmly on him, May hurried toward the cliff face and sheltered behind a boulder. The closer he came the more aware she was of his attire, or lack thereof. Tanned muscles flexed with every stroke of his oar, the contours of his lower arm muscles glistening in the last remaining rays of sunlight. Her breath caught. She'd never seen a man in such a state of undress. As a daughter of a viscount, the men she was usually introduced to were dressed in the height of fashion—knee breeches, waistcoats, jackets and cravats that oozed privilege and breeding.

Not this man it would seem.

May licked her lips the salty residue of the sea spray lingering on her tongue. When the prow hit the shallows, the man jumped into the water and pulled the boat onto shore. He looked around and started toward a cave that was once an old smugglers' den, which hadn't been used for many years, there were other caves that remained drier for such use on the next cove. In fact, her father could only remember it used sporadically when he was a boy.

But the land the stranger was now on wasn't a public beach. It was owned by her father, Viscount Levinstone, and this smuggler, pirate or curious sailor was encroaching on their property. Anger thrummed through her veins, and forgetting her own safety, May stood to show herself. "You there. What's your business here?"

He paused mid-stride and ran a hand through his hair, pushing long sea swept locks from his forehead. Again, she struggled to control her breathing. He was like a male water nymph, with his wet shirt clinging to the contours of his chest and abdomen. A very rippled, perfect abdomen... She swallowed. Had he come to seduce women with his good looks.

May waited for him to respond to her question, and heat bloomed from her toes to her face as he travelled his insolent gaze down the length of her form. She bit her lip, hating the fact that having his attention on her made her nerves tremble and her stomach flutter, nothing like she'd ever experienced before.

"What is yours?"

His deep English accent, clipped and well tutored startled her out of her musings over what his legs may look like out of the breeches he wore. "This is my land. You're trespassing. So unless you wish the local magistrate to deal with you and your crew, you had better explain why you're here."

He laughed, the deep raspy sound was there again to tempt and lure. Of course she'd heard men laugh before, but this man actually sounded as if he found whatever she said genuinely funny, not false to appease a possible future bride. She glared, finding no mirth in her reaction to him. Never had she been so out of sorts with a man before, certainly no one raised such delectable butterflies in her stomach during her Season.

"Explain. Now." His knowing smirk sent odd warmth spreading to her stomach.

"I'm William Scott, Earl of Grandison. I was expected here today by Viscount Levinstone. He's an old friend of my father's."

May frowned. She'd never heard her father speak of him before. Odd. For all she knew, he could be a liar, a cutthroat wanting to kill them all, steal what little they had in their home. "And you're going to present yourself to my father dressed as you are?" She studied his ratty clothing, or at least very ratty pants, a dull brown that hardly fit the title of earl he declared to be.

He shrugged. "As you see."

"You're not fit to be seen." She paused. "How do I know you're not some scoundrel pirate who's masquerading as lord what's-his-name only to kill or steal from my family?"

"You will have to trust the word of a gentleman." His grin was devilishly handsome.

Damn the man. "Gentleman? You think me a fool?"

"I would never presume such." The chuckle that followed his words only indicated he did indeed find her a little foolish and one to be trifled with. "Shall we?" He raised his eyebrows and gestured toward the house.

May narrowed her eyes. "Give me some proof you know my father." She paused. "Describe his appearance."

"Well," he frowned, "he's a short, bald man, rotund, seems to like his desserts a lot. He's a kind, considerate and trusting man. The last three traits would not go astray with you, if you don't mind my saying."

She shut her mouth with a snap. "I beg your pardon. Who are you to tell me what to do or how to act? I'll have you know I'm going to be a nun in only a few weeks. A woman who will show mercy, kindness, and godliness, much like the pope." To be chastised by someone who knew her not at all wasn't to be borne. How dare he.

He crossed his arms, smiling. "Really? You're going to be a woman of the cloth?" He laughed. "Perhaps I'll stick around long enough to see that."

"You think I would lie about my future situation? I would never do such a thing." And as for explaining what her father looked like, she was loath to admit he'd described him perfectly, maybe even a little too perfectly. "You speak about my father as if you've seen a painting and are copying it from memory. Now we'll just wait and see if he remembers you or if you, Lord Grandison, are the liar."

May marched back toward the estate and left the earl-turned-sailor standing on the beach. The distance that opened up between them did little to relieve the blasted nerves assailing her every time she looked at him. Or the fact she could feel his gaze marking her back like a scorching flame. She fought her body's ridiculous reactions to the man and turned her mind to how much he'd annoyed her. How dare he say she was inconsiderate? There was nothing wrong with her. She was one of the nicest people she knew. Even if she had to say so herself.

Will watched Viscount Levinstone's daughter storm toward the manor house. It reminded him of a ruffled peacock, similar to the birds on his estate when, as children, he ran after them, teasing relentlessly.

She didn't turn back and he followed the little minx. To become a nun as she'd stated she'd want to work on her manners. He doubted the good nuns who devoted themselves to God would take kindly to a fellow member of the church who looked down on strangers as unwanted and untrustworthy people without even knowing a thing about them. Not to mention failing to introduce herself.

Not that he was always so trustworthy. His family would state he was anything but. A chilling wind pierced his shirt and Will shivered. As the head of the family, he supposed they had little choice. Unfortunately his hasty departure following the announcement in his father's will of his arranged betrothal to a woman he did not care for or love, did nothing to endear him to his mother or siblings.

He would be lucky if they ever spoke to him again. Will sighed. He'd not meant to embarrass his betrothed

Mary, but they were ill-suited and their marriage would never have worked. That she felt the same as he, and had in fact since married the man she was in love with, didn't sway his family's disgust at his actions. They still refused to see sense and had merely lifted their already lofty noses in the air whenever he returned home. William had sought refuge in London, and had thrown himself into politics, which eventually led him into the position he now held. He'd always loved the ocean, and having accompanied one raid on a smuggling ring in Kent, his life finally had purpose.

Each time he stepped onto the wooden deck of a ship, smelt the salt in the air, and the taste of adventure to come, he'd never felt more at home, more at ease. The tide had turned in his favor, his course had been set and he hadn't looked back.

Of course, he'd continued to look after his estates from afar, the guilt of disappointing his family irked, but he refused to fail his tenants and farmers. It wasn't in his nature to be looked upon as untrustworthy and flippant. He was neither and hearing the little minx before him state as much sat ill in his gut. He would have to change her mind about what she thought of him…

The idea of such a challenge sent a thrill through his blood. The future nun would be an enjoyable distraction while he waited for his ship to return after undergoing repairs in London, and would also help pass the time until he was due to leave. He'd never met a woman so strong-willed, determined and fearless. And perhaps it was this independent will that made her more attractive to him than any other he'd ever met. May Stanford was certainly no demure, biddable miss who would bore him to death.

Will smiled. "I don't believe I've ever seen a house

more enjoyably situated. I would never wish to leave if I owned such a view. There is nothing better than the ocean, with its vastness and endless opportunities."

She looked back at him, and he read the wistfulness that darkened her eyes to a color he'd only seen in the deepest oceans, a blue so dark it was almost green. "I would have loved to travel the seas. But alas, as an unmarried female it isn't an option for me, no matter how much I may wish it." She pushed a lock of dark hair that fluttered against her cheek away and his fingers flexed as if it was he who had placed it back behind her ear. "I will have to content myself with my imagination, I'm afraid."

"There is nothing wrong with fantasizing." He grinned as her cheeks reddened into a pretty rose color. "I could always tell you a few tales that will satisfy your lust for adventure and will keep you warm on the cold nights in your convent cell, or should I say bed."

A disgusted huff released from between her quite full, delectable-looking lips—the one body part he'd noticed first after meeting her. They were supple and as red as the bloodiest rose. Will shook away the imagery that taunted him as to what she could do with such a pretty mouth.

That this future nun was beautiful, fiery and of his class could not go unnoticed or ignored. She may not like him very much now, but he could or would change that fact. He didn't like people thinking ill of him unless of course they had good reason to.

"I'll keep to my own imaginings if you don't mind, my lord. I don't need any fables from you."

Will cleared his throat, fighting not to laugh at her disgusted, most definitely insulted tone. "Well, if you change your mind, you only need to ask."

She shook her head and started for the house again.

Will fought the grin on his lips and lost. They entered the Tudor-style manor through the double, weather-worn front doors, the grey timber aged by salt and coastal winds. The foyer was large with a sweeping staircase up to the first floor landing. Walls were decorated with tapestries; armory and old oak furniture complimented the medieval feel of the home.

"This way," his lady companion said walking toward another front room Will thought may be the library. Instead, he entered a parlor that housed two settees and a large fireplace that dominated the quaint space. A small boy sat before the marble hearth playing knuckles and Viscount Levinstone sat watching, a proud, contented look across his face.

"Papa, we have a visitor." She stated, her eyebrows raised and looking at him as if he were a liar. "Do you know this gentleman?"

"William!" Viscount Levinstone shouted, jumping up from his chair. "Welcome! I'm so pleased you're able to join us. I know your pursuits on and off our great land keep you busy."

Will bowed. "I was honored to receive your missive, Lord Levinstone. Father often spoke fondly of his time here as a young man."

A chuckle ensued from his lordship reminding Will that his father and the gentleman before him had in fact been the typical Bond Street beaus with many a Banbury tale to share. The stories he'd heard put his days at Cambridge to shame.

"You know this man, Papa?" May asked, incredulous.

He grinned at his foe and reveled at the glare he received in return.

"Of course, my dear. This is Lord William, the Earl of

Grandison." His lordship smiled. "This is my daughter, May. I hope she has not been giving you a hard time of it." His lordship looked out the window toward the front drive. "As I heard no carriage arrive I assume you came via the sea?"

Will nodded. "I did, my lord. I fear I may have frightened your daughter into believing I was a ruffian or pirate about to plunder her home, especially as I'm not dressed properly to be received. I do apologize for my dishevelment. My bags are stowed in the small raft on the beach."

"Well, it would have certainly livened things up a bit had you been a pirate." His lordship walked over to his daughter and took her hand. "I promise you, my dear, Lord William is quite respectful and a very honorable gentleman. You have nothing to fear from him." His lordship turned his attention onto him. "I will send a servant down directly to pick up your things."

Will's gaze locked with May's. Such a sweet name that seemed at odds with the woman's temperament. Her eyes narrowed and his amusement over her dislike of him only increased his interest.

He smiled. Something told him he was going to enjoy the next few weeks and Christmas at the Viscount Levinstone's home. Enjoy it very much.

CHAPTER 2

For what felt like the hundredth time, May sat up and punched her pillow into something that resembled comfort. She flopped down on the cotton sheets that usually lulled her to sleep within moments, but tonight nothing seemed to be working.

"Blast it." She pushed off the blankets, grabbed her robe that lay at the end of her bed and headed for the door. The corridor was dark with only the smallest amount of moonlight lighting her way along the passage. Having lived here her entire life at least made the walk to the library downstairs an easy feat.

She jumped down the last step and headed for her father's sanctuary. Just inside the door a small lamp sat, its wick burning low, the servants not having yet completed their final check of the house before bed. May picked it up and strolled to the bookcase where her father kept her mother's favorite poems. She studied the authors' names for a moment, her mind at war with itself over what literature she was in the mood for. Love and romance, or misery and tempest…

"And so we meet again."

She gasped, twisting about, her heart beating a million times faster than it ought. "What are you doing down here? It's after midnight."

As soon as the words left her lips, she cringed. After midnight was probably nothing to this earl-turned-pirate-turned-captain-turned-nuisance. Not that he was a pirate, but May had no doubts some of his business dealings were anything but above water. Figuratively speaking.

He lifted the book he held in his hand and waved it at her. "Reading. What do you think I was doing?"

What did she think he was doing? All kinds of thoughts bombarded her mind, and none of them appropriate for a lady. He was here alone, and by the looks of his empty glass, probably foxed as well. Men of his ilk always held assignation's with women in darkened libraries, didn't' they? May pushed aside the thought that she was the only women in the house beside the servants.

His grin caught her full attention and she couldn't seem to shift her gaze from his lips. Her heart beat acceler-ated to an absurd crescendo and she frowned. "That, I would prefer not to answer, my lord." She looked back at the bookshelf and took a calming breath. With every word he spoke he seemed to be saying something other than what he meant. Vexing man.

She clasped a book she was neither interested in or knew much about. A creak sounded behind her followed by a thump. May swung about and immediately took a step back as Lord William stood before her, a towering lump of muscle and masculinity.

He reached for a book beside her head, his arm grazing against her shoulder and sending a delicious shivers to flutter in her stomach. May tried to ignore her reaction to him, and failed miserably. The scent of the sea mixed with soap emanated from him. William smelt clean, fresh and utterly forbidden to her. In only a few weeks, she would start her training as a nun. Her mind truly needed sanity right at this moment, certainly not impurity.

She swallowed, burying her reactions. She would be a simpleton indeed if she didn't react to a man in such a way. Women were, after all, made to join with them, marry and have children with the opposite sex. Just from this moment on, she would have to cure herself of such an infliction. A life with the church was only a few weeks away, she reminded herself. "Oh, umm…" she stuttered at her own musings. This man had trouble written all over him.

He grinned down at her, his azure eyes sparkling with mirth, as if privy to her most inappropriate thoughts and reactions to him. "I think you'll find these books most interesting, and although not what you'd normally look at, it may bore you enough that you'll sleep well."

May clasped the book without looking at the cover and pushed past the overbearing earl. She strode from the room without a backward glance and headed for her bedroom taking the stairs two at a time before making the sanctuary of her suite. After shutting the door, she snipped the lock and leaned against the wood. Her eyes widened as she gazed at the books she clasped tightly against her chest. What had he given her?

Memoirs of a Woman of Pleasure and some book that housed erotic engravings. Her father would kill her if he knew she had these in her room. May threw them onto the floor and crossed herself with the sign of the lord. Lord Grandison was a villain and possibly out to ruin her future as a nun. For God help her, staring at the books that lay on her Aubusson rug, she'd dearly love to read through them.

Her fingers itched to turn the pages, and see what she would forever be missing. Were the memoirs true? Was what was in the book possible between a man and woman?

She sighed and picked the books up with the notion she didn't want the maid to find them in the morning. Jumping into bed, she settled herself under the covers and opened the book of engravings. Her breath hitched and she bit her lip as a shiver slid down her spine. "Oh my." Never had she seen any drawings like these ones before. In fact, she hadn't even known her father had such books in his library.

May crossed her legs as warmth spread through her core. She studied the engravings which encompassed a couple in various positions during what she assumed to be the act of love making. She flicked through the book. Page after page revealed legs entwined, discarded gowns, and pants that were askew. She swallowed, heat blooming on her face. She had never imagined such things were even possible between two people. And yet it was the ecstasy on their visages that caught her attention the most. They were thoroughly enjoying what they were doing together.

She shut the book with a snap and getting out of bed, grabbed the second book and stashed them at the bottom of one of her drawers under shifts and gloves. The last thing she needed was her maid to find these kind of books in her room. The thought of the gentleman brought a rush of annoyance at his presumption not to mention gumption at giving her such items to read. Right now, he was probably laughing at her in his room knowing very well what she was looking at.

Well, two could play at his game. She was anything but a woman to push over as his lordship the pirate captain would soon find out.

· · ·

The next morning May sat at the breakfast table and nibbled on some toasted bread. An early riser, she ate alone, her father and brother still abed. Not that she expected to see them until luncheon, her father preferring to eat breakfast in his room since her mother's passing five years ago.

The door opened and the pirate captain himself strolled in with an air of authority. May felt her eyes widen and cursed her foolery. He was just a man. Annoying and too smart for his own good. She raised her brow and gave him the most severe stare she could muster. His resounding chuckle only strengthened her resolve to teach this man, who seemed to take up all the air in the room, a lesson he'd not soon forget. "Up and about already, Lord Grandison. I thought gentlemen of your ilk sleep most of the day away, only to create a ruckus all night. You'll confuse the servants if you keep up this regime."

He stood at the sideboard and poured himself a mug of coffee. "I should imagine if they find the books I gave you last night in your room, you'll cause a greater stir then any I ever could." He turned and smiled before taking a sip. "Have you looked at them yet?"

She refused to blush and silently thanked God when she didn't. "I did flick through the engravings." She took a sip of tea and fortified herself to play just as well as he at this teasing game. "Some of the positions looked a little fanciful to me. Do you think they're really possible?"

He sputtered and placed his coffee mug down with a clatter. May inwardly grinned. She met his gaze and held it. "All of them would be possible. Do not doubt it, my lady."

"I give you leave to call me May since you know my

family so well. And since you feel that such literature is appropriate for me to read, I'm assuming you wouldn't mind if I called you William? Since we're such close friends after just one day." May stated, her voice as sweet and innocent as she could muster.

He coughed but nodded. "Of course."

"There was one position I'm most interested in and would like your opinion of it, if you wouldn't mind? Perhaps this morning you could explain it to me, if you have time." William pulled at his cravat, his ratty attire of yesterday seemingly a thing of the past. Today he was dressed to the epitome of what a gentleman should look like. Pressed beige pantaloons and starched white shirt with accompanying cravat were finished to perfection with a dark blue claw-hammer coat.

A pang of disappointment assailed her over his abundant attire this morning. She'd enjoyed seeing him yesterday, or namely his ratty barely-there shirt that showed off his muscular frame. With any luck, her forwardness and determination to make him squirm after giving her such books would make the muscles beneath all that cotton and wool quiver and flex.

"I'm not sure if that would be appropriate. I should apologize for giving you such literature to read." He buttered a heated roll but wouldn't meet her gaze. "It was wrong of me, and I'm sorry."

May inwardly laughed. "Well, well, well, aren't we full of remorse today. How can you think such books would make me uncomfortable, especially knowing I'm going to be a nun very soon?" Sarcasm dripped from her every word and she was glad to see William shift uncomfortably on his chair.

He looked at her and pursed his lips. Her gaze locked

on them yet again, and she noted the lovely shape as he licked a droplet of coffee from the corner of his mouth. Not too thin or puffy, but just nice and what all lips should look like if she was going to be a lip connoisseur. "May?"

"Pardon?" She shook herself from her musings. "I'm sorry, did you say something?"

"You may bring the book into the billiards room before luncheon. We'll go through it then."

She felt the blood drain from her face. Without his usually teasing grin, William stood and left the room. May followed his every step until the door shut quietly behind him. She stared at the door a moment. Had she just walked into a trap and one of her own making?

Damn it. She swallowed. This was not how her morning was supposed to go.

Will ran a hand through his hair as he stormed toward a billiards room he'd seen the day before. He needed to smack a few balls around for an hour or so. Anything to take his mind off what he'd just invited May to do with him later. Of all things holy. How was he to discuss such a book without…Well without reacting like any virile young male would?

Shit!

He stopped at the threshold of the room and cursed anew. Spotting the billiard sticks, he clasped one and set up the table. A few minutes into his solitary game, Matthew, May's younger brother strolled into the room and watched him.

William smiled at the young lad who looked a little bookish and very pedestrian, if his highly starched shirt and clean pants were any indication. Unlike his sister, he surmised he didn't venture down to the sea shore too often. "Matthew, how are you today? Would you care to have a game with me?"

The young boy smiled but didn't venture any closer. "No, thank you. I don't like the game. If you ask my sister though, I'm sure she'll give you one. May's very good."

"Your sister plays billiards?" Why this pleased him to hear he had no idea, and in all truth it didn't surprise him. He was starting to surmise May did a lot of things well. Including driving him mad.

"Often. She always beats Papa and now he'll no longer play against her."

Will chuckled. He loved nothing more than a challenge together with a wager. Perhaps it could be his way of getting to taste, even just once, May's delectable lips. "Well, I'll have to ask her then."

Matthew nodded before turning on his heel and walking from the room. William smiled. What an odd little creature he was.

All too soon, May arrived, keeping her attention fixed firmly on the windows that looked over a native area of the garden, filled with coastal plants and manicured lawn walkways.

William sat down on a settee made for two and didn't say anything as she sat beside him. Her features weren't telling him anything new, other than the usual aloofness and disdain she held for him since their first meeting. "Are you ready for your lesson, my lady?"

Her eyes widened a fraction and it was the first glimpse he had of her that perhaps she wasn't as composed as she made out to be. Good. That made two of them. "Yes. And to make things easier I've marked certain pages I wish to discuss first."

Will took the book from her and braced himself to engage in the most inappropriate action of his life. He would burn in hell for what he was about to discuss with a future nun. He opened the book and an image of a man taking a woman from behind met his gaze. He inwardly cringed at having the task of explaining such a position. He really ought not to tease people into retaliation in future.

"This doesn't look at all possible to me. I think the artist is playing its readers for fools."

William cleared his throat. "This position is possible and enjoyable for both parties." He ran his finger over the image to where the man and woman joined. "The woman would—" The word stuck in his throat and May looked at him expectantly. "Would encounter deeper penetration and probably reach orgasm quite quickly, especially if the man reached around and touched the woman's most private of places."

"Most private of places?" May stated, her eyes widening in alarm.

William cringed. "It's a little nubbin that can be stimulated to make the woman orgasm."

"Oh, well, that's very interesting." Her cheeks went bright red and William cursed himself a fool for ever giving her the books in the first place.

William took a calming breath. "Do you know of what I speak?" His body hardened as he waited for May's reply, and as much as he fought to keep it under control, the thought of them in the exact poses in the books, drove him to distraction. That he was feeling this way without a single touch from her upon his person was telling indeed.

"Oh...I—" Her mouth formed a perfect O and he forced himself to look at the painting hanging across the room. He didn't need any more imaginings of what her mouth in that shape could do to him. He cringed at his own thoughts. He was a cad.

Will took pity on them both and shutting the book, he said, "I believe we should stop reading through these together. I'm not sure what your stance is on the matter, but I'm finding this extremely uncomfortable." Pleasurable yes, but painful. Will adjusted his seat, hoping May didn't notice his growing arousal.

She let out a relieved sigh. "I'm glad you said so, as I am as well." She laughed, the sound making his gut clench pleasantly. "I just couldn't let you think you could disconcert me like you did."

"I don't know what I was thinking." Will met her gaze, holding out his hand. "Let us shake on a truce and work on being friends?"

May's delicate fingers entwined with his and heat coursed up his arm. "That sounds perfect. Thank you," she said.

Will pulled away and sat back. "You know, I must admit I enjoy liberating conversation as the one we've just shared. It's not often that a lady and a gentleman can talk so frank."

"It was, wasn't it?" She paused, a small frown between her perfect eyebrows. "I'm sorry for how I treated you when we first met. I was very unkind and rude."

He waved her concerns away, not liking the worry that clouded her blue orbs. "Should the positions have been reversed, I would have been wary as well. You were right to question me as you did. You are a strong, willful woman who only wishes to protect her family. That is something to be commended."

"Thank you." For the first time since he'd met her, she looked at him with warmth.

William couldn't sever their locked gazes even if he wished to. There was something innocent and wicked about May that drew him like a moth to a flame, and even knowing that his wings would be burned should he get too close, it would not stop him. "You're a very beautiful woman. Is your heart really set on becoming a nun?"

The luncheon gong sounded and both of them jumped back. He chuckled feeling absurdly young and innocent, which he was not. His years enjoying town life had ensured his innocence was lost many years ago. "I suppose we should go."

She stood quickly and stood there a moment before looking back at him. "I have my reasons for wanting to enter the church. Life is complicated and unfortunately we do not always get what we want or with the passing of time, what we want changes."

His eyes narrowed at the resolve he heard in her voice. What did May really want? He doubted she always had her heart set on entering the church. And what a waste of a great woman should she end up doing so. Women such as May were rare gems that didn't come about in society often. It baffled him how she'd not found a husband in town. She was a Viscount's daughter, from a good family and home. Her choice made little sense to him.

There was nothing left to it, he would have to try and change her mind.

CHAPTER 3

May took a calming breath and strolled toward the dining room, noting that the servants were busy decorating the house with holly and mistletoe. The deep red and green ribbons they were wrapping about the staircase banister brought home even more that Christmas wasn't far away, and very soon her life at home would be over.

She could hear her father and brother talking upstairs as they made their way downstairs. Her heart pounded and had the lunch gong not sounded, she was sure William may have kissed her. Her first real kiss. Pleasure thrummed throughout her body, causing goosebumps to rise on her skin. Dressed as a gentleman today, he really was very pleasant looking. And when speaking to her like an equal, not a silly, young woman, it made him even more appealing.

At the dining table, she sat at her usual spot and greeted her family as they entered. William followed and he grinned. May smiled back as he settled himself across from her.

"I thought with your permission, Lord Levinstone, I could steal away your daughter for the afternoon and have her show me the estate. I understood from Father it's quite vast."

May choked on her slice of ham and took a sip of water. "You want to see the estate? With me?" She vaguely heard her father's answering chuckle and ignored it. "Why?"

"Why wouldn't anyone wish to see your home? I'm sure it is magnificent with its wild beauty and rugged shorelines."

Her father nodded eagerly, a large smile on his face. "Of course May will show you around. I look forward to hearing about your excursion tonight at dinner."

"Papa, we haven't anyone to chaperone us. I cannot go." She quickly met William's challenging gaze. He looked different from when they were together in the private parlor, as if he was contemplating something that involved her in his stormy blue eyes. May ignored her rioting emotions at the thought of them being alone and away from the house... This was dangerous.

Her father sighed. "We are not in London now. No need to stand on ceremony. And I trust your judgement, May, no matter what you may think." He threw her a pointed stare. "Lord Grandison is also a guest. He would not displease me. Would you, my lord?"

"Of course not," he stated, nodding once. "And please, call me William. No need to stand on ceremony between friends."

May turned to a waiting footman. "Please send word to the stables for two horses to be saddled directly."

The footman bowed and left to do her bidding. She ate the rest of her lunch in silence, the conversation of farming the least of her thoughts. All that occupied her mind was that for the next few hours she was going to be alone with a man. And not just any man, but the only man who made her uncomfortable in all the right places on her body.

This was a dreadful conundrum.

A little while later, May rode Mystic, her Arabian mare, out of the stable yard at a trot. She refused to give way to the urge to roll her shoulders from William's direct gaze that bore into her back.

He'd been quiet as they'd mounted their horses. Words threatened to bubble out of her, asking him what he was thinking in that bold mind of his. Or why on earth he wanted to look around an estate that farmed mostly sheep and little else. Even baby lambs after a few years were not that exciting to look at.

She pointed out some landmarks, the local church and the direction of the closest town as she rode along an old coastal path, known only by the few estate workers. Cliffs gave way to sandy beaches and the view of the ocean called to her to explore and enjoy. Just as it always had since she was a little girl.

"Do you own all this land?"

The question started her out of her musings and she pulled her mount to a stop. "Yes. The beach below is very good for fishing. There are some old smuggler caves there as well."

"Can you show me?"

"If you wish it." She dismounted and tethered Mystic to a nearby tree. William did the same and followed her as she showed him the way down to the beach. Grey, angry storm clouds gathered on the horizon and May paused. "I'm a little worried about the weather." The wind picked up and the sweet, fresh scent of forthcoming rain accompanied it.

William gazed past her and narrowed his eyes. "You might be right. How long would it take for you to show me the smuggling caves?"

"Not very long, but the weather can come in quickly here. I'm not sure if we should risk it, it's quite a steep climb to the shore." She took another glance at the gathering clouds. "Oh well, come on. As long as we don't dawdle, we should be all right."

"Dawdle?" William laughed. "Now that's something I haven't done in a while."

May headed for the worn walking trail. No doubt he never dawdled. He was probably too busy with numerous women to ever think about taking some time to just enjoy their company instead of their bodies. Although, after the images she'd seen in those books, enjoying women as he did, he probably enjoyed life immensely. May sighed, not knowing how she felt about such thoughts.

They reached the sand, and with the increased wind, the waves swirled and broke higher against the shore than normal.

"Just over here they are." She entered one smuggling cave. "Now where did I leave the lamp?" she mumbled to herself.

"You have a lamp here?"

The question asked quite near her back made her start. In the dark, she supposed William hadn't known how close he was to her. The thought that he knew exactly how close she was and what his nearness did to her nerves wasn't worth thinking about. "I used to play in most of the caves along this shore and others. I left lamps in all of them. I can't see in the dark, you see," she said, lighting it quickly.

He laughed and stepped closer still. "Do you realize you just made a joke?"

"I may be a future nun, my lord, but I'm not dead. I do know how to enjoy myself."

"Really?" A disbelieving eyebrow rose. "How?"

"I do all manner of things. None of which you need to know about." The thought of what she would like to do, with this man especially was enjoyment enough. And it was all his lordships fault in any case. Had he not shown her those naughty books, she would never have had any of these thoughts haunting her mind.

May stilled when he placed a stray curl behind her ear, his fingers lingering to slide down her neck.

"What if I'd like to know? Would you tell me?"

His voice was low, and the breath of his words brushed her ear, leaving heat to pool at her core. The flickering flame cast a shadow across his face making him look like the rugged man she'd first met on the beach. "Probably not." Her whispered voice sounded breathless with need. Had she known better she would assume William was courting her right at this moment. Seducing her even.

"What if I begged?" His touch glided down her arm and she shivered at the roughness of his palm.

"You shouldn't touch me like that." May made no move to remove his hand and she knew her statement was moot. She did want him to touch her like that, and in a lot of other places not just her arm. If only she could blame the books entirely, but she could not. After her disastrous Season in town, where she'd seen many of her friends find husbands, and noted the many stolen kisses they partook in, May had wanted to experience the same. It looked so delicious to be held against a man's body, to have them want you with a desperate need that matched your own.

Slowly he leaned down and brushed his lips against hers. "I want to touch you. Desperately."

His gaze searched hers and she read the question he held inside. Would she allow his kiss? Oh, yes, absolutely. If only once before entering the church. May reached up and pulled him against her mouth. Their lips meshed and held and on a gasp his tongue swept against hers with abandonment.

The need to enjoy every moment and place everything they were doing in her memory urged her to follow his lead. Tentatively she flicked her tongue against his. The oddest sensation, one she'd never felt before bombarded her senses. Heat, soft flesh against flesh, a mating of mouths ensued. Her stomach clenched in desire and she closed the space between them completely.

William's hand slipped about her waist and slid down to pull her against him. She gasped as the hardness she recognized as his manhood stood against her body. He wanted her. Wanted her as much as she craved the touch of him.

The stone wall of the cave met her back as he pushed her up against it. He broke the kiss and May felt a slight chill as he lifted the hem of her gown. She bit her lip as William slowly kissed his way down her neck and across the bodice of her down.

"We should stop." William pulled back a little. "I promised your father."

May inwardly cursed. They couldn't stop now. Her body craved him, needed him. This was possibly her only chance of ever experiencing such a tryst with a man and having the memory to keep her warm for many years to come. Determined to get her way, she slipped her hand about his member and stroked. "No. I forbid it."

He growled as more air swept across her thighs. She closed her eyes, hoping William might touch her where she now thrummed in pleasure. It was wrong. So deliciously wrong, but so good as well. If only to experience this once in her life, she would be content.

"Just say the word and I will stop," he said.

May couldn't bring herself to say anything. She clasped the hair at his nape and brought him back to her mouth just as the feather-light touch of his hand skimmed over her most private of places. She moaned. His kiss deepened, their tongues entwining with force as his fingers, one in particular slid across her nubbin. May wrapped her leg about his hip and William took advantage of her action and parted her undergarments. Moisture pooled at her core, her body craving his touch. He stroked her heat, flicked over the part of her that ached for more.

"Can you remember what this part is called," he asked, making her whimper with longing as his hand sent another burst of pleasure to course through her blood. "Do you want me to show you what it can do?"

Without heed, May undulated against his hand. "It's called a nubbin and yes, please show me what it can do."

William smirked flicking her smart little nubbin again, and then he did something she'd never thought possible. He slid one and then two fingers into her and there was no stopping her moans as he worked her heated flesh toward pleasure. With each stroke, he kissed her, his tongue mimicking what his hand was doing beneath her gown. This was so much more than she'd ever imagined and realization hit her that *this* was why women married men. Who would not want to enjoy such touch every day.

"You're so beautiful. I want you, May. I want to taste your sweet body more than you'll ever know," he said, his voice rough with need.

Would she go to hell for enjoying herself so much? Probably, but right at this moment she couldn't bring herself to care. May made a mental note to pray for forgiveness for her sin when she arrived at the convent. "I know…" She sighed as pleasure mounted and her body burned in his arms.

William rubbed her button and kept up his relentless invasion. May rocked toward his touch, her need for more of what he could give her overriding all decorum and lady-like manners she ought to have.

"Hell, yes. I want you to come."

She met his gaze, his eyes large and luminous in the flickering lantern light. "Come?"

"Orgasm," he said, stimulating her once more. "Pleasure, absolute pleasure."

May grinned, but agreed to do whatever he wished, especially if the things he did to her felt this good, like her body was not her own, and something marvelous was about to happen that she didn't yet know existed.

She held on to his shoulders, the muscles beneath his clothing taut and flexing with every stroke he bestowed on her wanting body. He kissed her again, making her dizzy and yet a part of her realized he wasn't experiencing anything like she was right now. All this attention was just for her. Determined to remedy the shortfall, May glided her hand down his chest, enjoying the feel of a man beneath her. His stomach was tight and flat, his breathing fast and getting quicker the further her hand moved toward his breeches. Finding what she was looking for, May clasped his hardness and reveled in the startled gasp from him. "Do you enjoy it when I touch you this way?"

He slowed his strokes upon her flesh and met her gaze. "Very much so."

William swallowed the desire to lift May onto the ledge to the side of them, push her skirts further up her body and take her sweet, hot core in one thrust. His body roared with need. Hunger to make her his clawed at his very soul. He wanted her, more than he'd ever wanted any other woman before in his life. Her frankness in his arms, her enjoyment and innocence pulled at his heart.

The thought should scare him and yet it didn't. For even with all of May's ideas over the future she thought she craved, what they were doing together right now only proved to him it would be mortal sin to place her in a church married to the almighty God. The pliant, sexually awakening woman in his arms who waltzed with him so deliciously in the most sexual of ways would never last in a convent. It would be a sin indeed to hide such a treasure behind robes and prayer.

And he was determined to ensure she altered her ideals and instead, saw him as her future. To walk away from a woman who was smart, well educated and easy to speak with while also making the blood in his veins sing, would be absurd. She was kind, loving and passionate young woman. A prize too precious to leave behind when he sailed.

The thought of settling down and marrying May ought

to scare him, but it did not, if anything, the idea left him calm.

He increased the pressure to her sweet nubbin with his thumb, while he worked his finger relentlessly inside her. She panted, her body riding him as he dreamed she would. Just the thought of her riding his cock made him dizzy. The wetness coating his fingers proof she'd been aching for a man's touch for too long.

And not just any man's touch—his.

Her fingers bit into his skin, her body tightening about him and he could feel how close she was to release. Each sigh and labored breath dragged him deeper within her enthralling spell. Then with a hiccup of a sigh, she convulsed about him and shattered in his arms.

"That's it. Enjoy me." William nipped her chin and kissed her, milking every last tremor from her body. In the shadowed light, her eyes glistened with awakening and enjoyment. He smiled. "You're so beautiful. I wish to make you do this every day for the rest of your life."

She sat back a fraction, her bottom lip clasped between her teeth, her cheeks flushed. "I should feel embarrassed and ashamed of myself, but I cannot. I had no idea it could be like that between a man and woman."

William grinned. "It can be a lot better than that. I assure you. And when you're ready, I can show you if you like."

May pushed his hand away and settled her skirts, before adjusting her bodice. "While I did enjoy our encounter, I don't believe we should go any further. Our lives are going in two different directions, and while what you just showed me was amazing, I don't want to risk getting with a child."

William stepped away and adjusted his engorged cock

so not to scare her entirely. He had another three weeks or so before his departure, and she may not think an encore of what they'd just shared was necessary, but he had time to change her mind and make her see sense.

There was so much to explore, to see, do and visit in the world, and although he'd not known this woman for long, to know she'd missed out on life cocooned in a convent just wouldn't suit. He wanted to show her a life she could only ever dream about, but make it her reality. "Of course." He smiled. "Whatever you think is best."

CHAPTER 4

May sat at the table the following morning, her body relaxed and still sated after her brush with William the day before. Just the thought of what they'd done together threatened to make her blush.

Again...

In the quiet comfort of her room after leaving William and unable to rein in her desires, she had touched herself just as he had. It was no stretch to her imagination to imagine the hands stroking her flesh were William's. And although she'd not experienced the same powerful release she'd enjoyed in his arms, it was a pleasurable experience.

And one she hoped would happen again, for it certainly would not after she'd taken her vows to God. May sighed, not sure what she was feeling about her impending future. As much as the nuns were lovely and very welcoming to her at the convent, William had shown her a side of life that she'd never thought to see, to experience. And to walk away from such a future, was no longer as easy as she thought.

Her attention snapped to the clock. Would William be

joining her this morning? Just as if the thought had conjured him, the breakfast room door opened and he entered. His greeting smile brought forth hers, and she watched transfixed as he selected his meal from the sideboard, giving her a lovely view of his backside in freshly pressed breeches.

The memory of what his firm, perfectly shaped bottom felt like the day before left a delicious twist in her stomach. May reached for her tea, needing to something, anything than ogle the man.

William settled beside her, reached for his linen napkin and placed it in his lap. A single finger glided over the top of her thigh and she stilled, not expecting the touch. "Did you sleep well?" he asked, eating as if his hand was not currently playing with her person.

The blood in her veins boiled and warmth burst upon her cheeks. May met his gaze, the fieriness from his eyes all the poof she needed as to what he was thinking, wanting to do with her. She swallowed. "I slept very well. Thank you." She cleared her throat, hating the fact he knew very well by her breathless tone he'd affected her.

Cursing her inability not to be affected by him, she asked, "Why is your hand upon my leg?"

He shifted closer, and the fresh scent of soap teased her senses, not to mention the thought of William being naked… May reveled in his presence. William had a lovely complexion for a man, a healthy tan color she could only dream of having. Her coloring was a pasty white shade. Some thought it a lovely English Rose hue. May had always thought it made her looked washed out like a ghost.

"I like it there. I like how when I touch you here," he stroked her through her gown at her most private of places, "you tremble, your eyes widening as your breath hitches. I love that you react to me in this way."

May bit her lip but kept her gaze locked on him. His movements remained unseen by the staff due to the large linen table cloth covering their lower bodies, but still, it was scandalous, and marvelous too. "I like that I react this way to you too."

He sat back. The sudden emptiness within her at the loss of his touch frightened her. She shouldn't be so reliant on him. He would be gone in a month and so would she. But she couldn't get enough of him. In truth, couldn't stop thinking about him and what could be.

William's hands clenched on top of the table. "It is taking all my will not to lift you up, place you in front of me and take you here and now in front of everyone. I want you." He growled the last and she shut her eyes to stop herself acting on his desire.

The breakfast room door opened with a bang and May was startled back into reality. She needed to remember who and where they were. Her father with his concerns over the estate's lack of finances did not need his daughter creating a scandal that would bring shame on him in their small community.

"I didn't expect to see you up so early, Papa. What has brought you down this morning?"

He smiled and waved a newspaper at her. "I received the weekly news, my dear. I wanted William's opinion on an investment I read about."

May listened as the gentleman proceeded to discuss said investment along with the latest on-dits in the society pages. She was thankful for the distraction and opportunity to escape since she'd finished breakfast before William had arrived.

May stood and excused herself. She knew what she had to do. She had a little over three weeks left at her ancestral home. It was time she enjoyed herself as a woman before entering the church. She doubted William was looking for a wife, but a lover she had no doubt he would be agreeable to.

And maybe she would as well if their time together yesterday was any indication.

She strode toward the billiard room and paused to look at the small closet that sat nestled beneath the staircase. A wicked idea entered her mind and she made a snap decision to act upon her thoughts instead of mulling them over as she was wont to do and thus thinking herself out of exciting situations altogether.

She entered the small space but left the door ajar. William always played billiards after breakfast, so hopefully today wouldn't be any different.

Heavy steps sounded before the stairs and May peeked into the hallway. A grin formed on her lips seeing William headed her way. Noting no one else about, she let herself be seen and then stepped back inside. The pause in step and the widening of William's eyes she'd caught before going out of sight made her smile.

He joined her a moment later and closed the door. Only a modest amount of light penetrated the space, just enough to see body forms, but no features. Excitement, trepidation and need thrummed through her and made her squirm. "What are you doing, May?"

She stepped forward, no longer willing to miss the one opportunity she had with a man. In a convent, it was assured nothing like this would ever happen to her and during her Season in town, it most certainly had not. May skimmed her hands up his arms, his body taut as if ready to pounce. Was it too much to hope he would pounce and devour her?. "I want you too," she said, finally answering the statement he had made at breakfast.

William forced himself to control his breathing. The four words he'd ached to hear finally left lips he hungered to taste. Had it only been yesterday since he'd pleasured her? It seemed like an eternity. He dragged May the rest of the short distance that separated them and kissed her. Hard. There was no slow seduction. No stopping how he felt for her or showing through touch what she did to him.

Makes me burn and as grow hard as hell.

He ran his hand into her hair, spilling the tightly woven coiffure to cascade down her back. She gasped for air, and he nipped her chin enjoying the moan of encouragement his action brought forth. He scooped her into his arms and placed her on the small wooden table he could only just see in the darkened space. Without letting her think better of what they were about to do he spread her thighs wide, stepped between them and slid her gown slowly up to her waist.

A shiver rocked her body, but she didn't halt his progress. Desire tainted the air, along with a scent that encompassed May entirely—roses, sweet and beautiful.

William stood. "Lean back on your hands for me and just enjoy. Do you trust me enough to do that?"

He felt her nod, before she said, "Of course."

She did as he asked and he pulled her morning gown down past one breast and took her puckered nipple between his lips. She moaned as he flicked the beaded flesh with his tongue. His cock hardened more and he wanted to thrust into her welcoming heat and make her his.

Instead, he continued to kiss and tease her without touching any other part of her body. May writhed beneath him and he inwardly smiled. Her pants, soft moans and sighs drove him to distraction. He could listen to her decadent sounds for the rest of his life and never get bored. He released her nipple with a pop and pulled her pantalets over her slim hips and down her legs, exposing her to his hungry gaze. William lifted one foot and kissed along her leg. May shook in his arms, her hunger for him matching his. He reached her thigh and licked the softest skin he'd ever felt.

"What are you doing to me?" She whispered, threading her fingers through his hair.

"Everything I can," he said, truthfully.

May tensed in his arms, and it wasn't hard to know why. Somehow she'd figured out what he wanted to do, and yet, she remained seated, her legs spread and open to him like a sweetmeat on a plate.

William growled as he tasted her for the very first time. Unable to deny himself her essence a moment more, he flicked his tongue over her hooded button and stroked her mons, slow at first, his need to tease and bring her slowly to climax as important to him as the reason why he was here in Cornwall to begin with. "I want you to enjoy me, May. I never want you to forget our time together." He stood and claimed her lips. She kissed him with matching fire, her tongue no longer hesitant but demanding, commanding as his. William's body hardened to the point of pain and he slid his hand down her stomach, across her curls and into the sweet moist heat between her thighs.

She moaned as he pushed a finger inside her tight

passage. "Do you like that?" he asked, repeating the strokes over and over again.

"Yes," she panted, pulling him closer still. "What you do to me is truly...enthralling."

"I have plenty more enthralling to show you yet, beautiful." William kneeled and added his mouth to where his fingers stroked. The flick of his tongue upon her flesh along with his touch, relentlessly teased her. And he couldn't stop. The delightful gasps, the bite of her fingers splayed throughout his hair, holding him hostage against her flesh was the only place he wished to be.

"William," she moaned. "Don't stop." She lifted herself a little and undulated against his mouth.

"Yes," he said. "Take your pleasure. I want you to come."

Her movements became frenzied, her gasps louder, but he couldn't tell her to stop or quieten. She was a hidden gem among the unforgiving landscape that was Cornwall and one he intended to enjoy for as long as she would allow him. Her body convulsed about his fingers and he made love to her with his mouth. May fell apart in his arms, her orgasm long and fulfilling if her heightened breathing, and soft continual moan was anything to go by.

William stood and settled the hem of her gown. He took a deep breath, his cock throbbing with unsated desire. "Next time I will take my pleasure as well. Do you agree?"

She clasped his sounders and pulled him close. "If you don't take me soon, William, I may be forced to act in an even more unladylike manner."

He chuckled. "You promise?"

She kissed him, long and deep. "Oh yes, that I promise."

CHAPTER 5

May checked that the hallway was clear. Only a few candlelit sconces upon the wall burned at the late hour. She left her door ajar instead of closing it to save even the slightest sound that could result in her being discovered.

The house was quiet, only the sounds of the distant ocean crashing over the shore thrummed from outside. Good. She didn't need anyone awake to see her stealing away at this late hour.

May padded down the stairs and left through the kitchen door. A well-worn path led down to a cove she hadn't shown William on the day they went riding. She turned to look back at the house to be certain no one followed. Satisfied she was alone, she continued on. A flicking light of a ship off the coast told her what she needed to know—Stephen had arrived with the second-to-last shipment.

She made her way to the cave partially hidden with sea greases and vines. Pulling them aside, she thanked the lord for the moonlight and found her lantern just inside the entrance. May lit it quickly, and shone it facing the vessel. She then sat and waited for Stephen to come ashore. She only had one more shipment to store for them after this one, and her time as a smuggler would be over. She would miss this life and the thrill she always received when the blunt they so desperately needed changed hands. Smuggling may be against the law, but when needs must...May had done what she must.

A slight breeze blew in from the ocean and she shivered. Stephen had never told her what it was he was smuggling, but she assumed it to be sugar, lace or alcohol of some kind. Whatever it was, it didn't matter to her. All that mattered was the money that would come in handy for her brother's future and the care of an estate she loved just as much as her sibling.

A small wooden craft slid onto the shore and Stephen jumped out, the usual group of men following him toward the cave. "Good evening, Stephen," she said, shaking his hand, their usual response whenever they met.

"May." He bowed and gestured for his men to enter the cave. "I trust all is well here."

"Yes, very well." She stepped away from where the men were stacking the crates and met Stephen's gaze. "One more shipment and we're done. Correct?"

"Right ye are. One more." He handed over an envelope and May placed it into the pocket of her cloak.

"I can't say I won't miss our interludes, but I shall miss the money."

Stephen laughed. "Always forward. I like that in a woman."

She blushed but smiled. "Thank you. I'll take that as a compliment."

He shifted his feet, no longer able to meet her eyes and

she hoped she'd not embarrassed one of her oldest childhood friends. The thought made her laugh. "Hurry lads. We've not got all night."

"Well," she said, "I'll leave you to your endeavors. At the next full moon, our business arrangement is complete."

"As agreed. And it's been a pleasure doing business with ye."

"I'm not sure if it's been a pleasure, but it's certainly been financially gaining." May smiled. "When I'm in the village next I'll check in on your mama."

"Thank you. You'll send word if she's unwell?"

"Of course." She turned for home, and walked the steep climb to the top. The breeze pushed at her back and an odd sense shivered down her spine that she was no longer alone. May looked about but couldn't see anyone. With the moon so bright they would have to be hiding very well.

Shaking off the chill, she went back inside then to her father's den and left the envelope in his top drawer like she always had, every month for the last two years. And with one more payment her brothers future would be secure. Of course, he'll never be rich and will have to work hard to keep the estate running, but at least he will be starting his life debt free and with a little blunt put aside for safe keeping.

May slept late the following morning, but the smell of hot chocolate brought her out of her delightful dream of William and his deliciously naughty mouth. Tired from the night before, she had allowed herself to sleep in longer than normal. Stifling a yawn, May rolled over and gazed out over the ocean that was visible from her bed. From here, she could make out the distant emerald sea that sparked in the sunlight. A pang of sadness clutched at her heart. She would miss her home and everyone in it. She would miss this view.

Not to mention after being with William, she would miss him as well. In a month they would no longer be together, but away and living their respective lives. Not that she really knew what he did other than captain a ship and look after his estates from his office on the high seas.

May sighed. She shouldn't have allowed herself to experience anything with the gentleman. The moment his lips touched hers, she knew it would only make her time in the convent all the more painful to bear.

And that time she would have to endure until she died. It was a sobering thought and one she ought to think more on, before rushing off to procure a religious habit.

She slipped from the bed and dressed quickly. The need to see him again made her fingers fumble with her gown. Without waiting for her maid, May threw her hair up with an assortment of pins and left the room.

She found him hitting the billiard balls around the game table, the deep frown line between his eyes making him look fiercer than she'd ever seen him before. Her step faltered. Should she interrupt his game? Deciding she should, May said, "Good morning, William." She smiled as he looked up at her. Nerves skittered through her stomach when his frown did not dissipate. If anything, it intensified. "Are you well?"

"Well enough." He paused, using the billiard stick to lean against. "How was your night?"

May inwardly frowned, not liking his curt tone. "Adequate I suppose. How was yours?"

William's eyes narrowed, and May had a sinking feeling as to why she thought she wasn't alone the night before.

"The same. I took a little walk."

May smiled to hide her unease. "I should imagine it was quite cold out." She gestured outside and to the storm clouds that were starting to build up. It would be raining by tonight.

He shrugged, leaning back over the billiard table to take another shot. "Chilling, more like."

"Well, I shall leave you to your game." Taking a fortifying breath, she concluded William wasn't in the mood for company. "Have a good day," she said, heading to her father's study, not comfortable with how dejected she felt over his indifference to her. She found her father bent over his ledger, his lips moving as he silently tallied up the figures before him. "Papa, did you find the envelope I left for you last night?"

He looked up and gestured for her to shut the door. "I did. Thank you my dear. But I've also had William in here like a bear, growling about your nightly walks. I think he may believe you have a beau waiting for you. He was acting most strangely. Almost like a jealous husband."

Warmth spread up her neck and threatened to consume her cheeks. "I'm sure he was only concerned for my welfare. Don't read into his actions any further than that, Papa." May sighed in relief knowing why William was angry with her. An odd sense of pleasure formed in her chest that the gentleman was jealous over whomever he thought she was meeting. Thankfully, her smuggling secret was still that. A secret. "I just left Lord William in the billiards room. He was quite curt and I thought he may have found out about our arrangement with Stephen."

"No, I don't believe he knows and best that he doesn't. He's a peer of the realm. It wouldn't be wise for the high in the instep Londoners to know of our arrangement, especially since we've only one more shipment to secure before we're finished with it."

"That was my thinking." May stood and walked to the window and caught a glimpse of her brother darting down toward the beach where she'd first met William. "I'm glad our smuggling will be completed by the time I leave for the convent. These funds should give Matthew brighter prospects and without me hindering him, he may be able to look to the future with some joy."

Her father's chair scraped across the wooden floor before he came to stand beside her. "You're not still thinking of becoming a nun. Come May. You are not contrite, meek or mild. Please reconsider your decision."

"Do not ask this of me, Papa. My choice is made. I love Matthew and will do anything to secure his position as Viscount Levinstone when the time comes. I know it's hard for you to understand, but please try. My mind is quite set on the matter." She turned and left the room. It was no surprise to her she didn't fit the mould that would make up a nun, but marriage no longer held the lure it once had. Her first disastrous Season had put paid to that fantasy. And yes she may be enjoying the company of William, but she was nothing but a passing fancy to him, certainly not someone he would marry. He'd certainly not hinted at wanting her for a bride… And disappointing as that was, like most gentlemen she came to know while in the capital, money was required when entering the marriage state, and that was one asset May lacked most of all.

Much to her annoyance, William kept his distance from her for the next few days. His cold, and at times rude, manner—as if she was an errant child who didn't know what was best for her—irked to the point of her endurance. Had he just asked her where she'd gone she would have soon put his mind to rest that it wasn't to meet another gentleman. He may not have received the entire truth, but that was better than thinking the worst of her.

After everything they'd done together surely he wouldn't think she'd look to have fulfillment elsewhere. He may have brought out a side of her character that even she didn't know existed, but she wasn't a doxy. Anger churned in her gut after his chilling attitude at dinner. Well, enough was enough. It was time William owned what she was sure he felt toward her, and if May had to seduce the fellow to make him see his true feelings, then that is what she would do.

May paced in her room and waited to hear her father's bedroom door close before making her way to the guest wing and William's suite.

Once her father retired for the night, May crept along the passage floor, making sure to miss the floorboards that were want to squeak. Without knocking, she entered William's room. He lay on the bed, bare of everything except his breeches. His chest was all muscle, his stomach flexed as he sat up and her attention locked on it. She swallowed when she noticed the bulge at the front of his pants. He was beyond spectacular. "Good evening, William."

He didn't move, just watched her, his eyes growing dark with need, but his severe expression, still one that sent her nerves to jangle. Knowing his distance from her was due to jealousy made each step closer to the bed much easier than she thought. Had she not been so sure of his feelings, she would never have been able to be so bold.

"You shouldn't be here."

She tipped her head to the side and studied him. His gaze took in her bodiced chemise, his hands fisting against the sheets. "You shouldn't be here?" she repeated, mocking his words for what they were, a lie. "I thought it was time you took your pleasure as well, my lord."

His eyes flared and his swallow was almost audible. "You should leave before you cannot."

May lifted her chemise and pulled it over her head, letting it flutter to the ground. She knelt on the bed near his feet. "I know exactly what I'm doing and I've never been so sure of anything before in my life."

For the first time since she'd entered the room, he looked away. Dread lodged in her stomach like a rock that perhaps he'd tired of her after all, and that perhaps she'd been wrong in reading his coldness as jealousy. The thought was mortifying. "Do you not want me?" There, she'd asked what she feared most to voice. That he did indeed wish her to leave and never come back.

"Two nights past, who did you go out to meet? I saw you walk out into the night toward the beach. Why?" His voice was hard and the frown she'd grown to dislike was back between his eyes.

"You followed me?" May leaned back and fortified herself for the lie she had to tell. "I've lived here all my life. Why shall I not go for a stroll when I wish?"

"You went for a stroll. In the middle of the night and in November, mind you, and you wish me to believe that?" He shook his head, disbelief clouding his tone.

She did want him to believe it as it was partially true. "Papa knows of my whereabouts. You can ask him if you wish." May moved a little closer to the bed, wondering what else she could say to make him at ease. "I have not shared my body with another if that is what you're implying."

The muscles in his jaw flexed and she knew without question, he was angry with her. Maybe even jealous over the thought another man may find her attractive, not that any of them ever had. The woman in her purred with satisfaction that she'd made this virile, beautiful man long for her in such a way he didn't want to share her with anyone else.

William lay back on the pillows and placed his hands behind his head. His muscles bulged with the action and she bit back a sigh of pleasure. He was so handsome, the annoyance in his gaze slowly being replaced with desire. May crawled onto the bed in the most seductive way she knew how, and tried to look as if she knew what she was doing. Her gown gaped at the front, and William's attention snapped to her chemise. She fought embarrassment and instead tried to embrace life and the opportunity he'd afforded her since visiting them in Cornwall.

"I don't know what to think anymore," he said, simply. His voice was husky and breathless as if he'd run a mile along the beach. The sound of it sent a thrill to her core and heat threaded through her body.

"I do," she answered, straddling his hips, relaxing at little when he clasped her waist holding her atop him. "I think we should be together, William. Completely."

He ground himself against her and her body tightened in expectation. "From the first moment you lifted your defiant chin, I wanted you." He chuckled. "I still cannot fathom how it is you're not married?"

May shrugged. "No one ever asked," she said, pushing

away the pang of sadness her statement brought forth. Not wanting such a hard truth to leave her melancholy, May set out to seduce William instead. It was by far a more enjoyable notion then dwelling on her disastrous London Season. She clasped his jaw and kissed him, tasting the lingering flavor of brandy on his lips. "And I wanted you too, William, so very much." Moving across his hardness, she noted that his gaze turned molten at the action, and an overwhelming sense of wickedness took flight.

He growled. "Then you shall have your wish, my lady." William flipped her onto her back and she laughed at the surprisingly quick action. His intense gaze never left hers as he ripped the buttons apart of his breeches and pushed the pants to his knees.

May lifted her legs and wrapped them around his waist and he came down onto her slowly, his hand grazing along the skin of her thigh. She squirmed, wanting to feel him, needing him as much as she needed air. "Please hurry."

His jutting penis pressed upon her heat sending spirals of desire coursing through her blood. May bit her lip as expectation and fear of the unknown wrestled within her.

"Look at me," he demanded, placing a delicate kiss on her nose.

She did and could read the need that warred with his concern for her. "There is no going back after this. You realize that, do you not?"

That William, even at this point in their lovemaking would halt the inevitable and give her a choice, vanquished any lingering doubts she had. "Do you promise that my life will never be the same?" she said, gasping as he sheathed himself fully within her, making her whole.

W illiam groaned for he'd certainly died and was in heaven. "I promise." May looked up at him with awe, and he fought to gain control. The woman beneath him had him more rattled than he'd ever thought possible by the opposite sex. And none of it had anything to do with how perfectly he fit her, or that she was perfection personified.

May's touch ran up the muscles on either side of his spine, urging him to move and so he did. Small strokes at first, allowing her the opportunity to get used to him and his ministrations. It didn't take her long to gain her rhythm. Her long smooth legs wrapped about his waist, and she arched beneath him, a quick study to the art of sex. His body roared for release, to spill his life within her, and make her his for all time, but not yet. William wanted to hear her moans of pleasure, to have her shatter in his embrace.

His chest ached at the thought that in only a few short weeks, he would be leaving, that this beautiful, passionate woman would be entering the church and promising herself to a higher power. It was not to be borne.

She moaned and he smothered the sound with a kiss. She was a marvel and never had he met anyone so strong and capable as her. At every turn, she matched his desire and fired his blood to new heights. The slow strokes turned into frenzied thrusts. Her urging of him to continue, to never stop would've felled him had he been standing. "Oh, William. I never—"

Thought it would be like this? Neither did he. She was magic in his arms. Her mouth opened on a sigh, her eyes closed, the long lashes fanned against her perfect cheeks as her release pulsated around him. She was too beautiful, too lovely to ever give up without a fight.

He clasped her calf, hoisting her leg higher on his hip and thrust deep. Just as man was unable to hold back the tide, he was unable to hold back his release as it ripped through him. William reveled in the sound she made as tremor after tremor threaded throughout her core. Never had he heard such sweet music, and it was a tune he wanted an encore performance of.

They collapsed beside each other, their breathing rapid, and their skin cloaked in sweat.

May turned into his waiting arms and kissed his chest before laying her head in the crook of his arm. "Thank you. I'll never forget this night for as long as I live."

Male satisfaction made him grin although he was determined to remove the resolve he heard in her voice. There would be no settling for anything less than him if he had anything to do with her future. "I'm glad to hear it." William pulled her close, wanting to hold onto this moment forever. "You know, now that I've had you, you'll never get rid of me."

He felt her smile against his chest. "That's good. Because I don't want to be rid of you just yet either. If that book you gave me is any indication, there are a lot of other...positions to try."

William looked down and met her laughing gaze. "What positions?"

"All sorts of positions." Her finger circled his nipple and his cock flexed, ready and eager for more. "You'll be a busy man, I believe, if we're to experience the whole book."

He growled and pulled her to straddle him. Right at this moment, he would do whatever May wished and it was no hardship to lay with her in his arms, make love to a woman who'd captured his heart and soul. "Where have you been hiding all my life?"

Her features sobered. The desire of a moment before was replaced with a sadness he wanted to eliminate from her world. "Here." She shrugged. "But just too insignificant for anyone to notice."

Well, he'd noticed, and he cared more than he ever thought possible after such a short time. "Not anymore you're not."

CHAPTER 6

May sat on the beach and kicked off her slippers. Her brother tiptoed in the shallow water before her, scrunching up his nose whenever the water lapped at his feet. This time of year it was beyond chilly, but having grown up here, they still liked to enjoy the water as much as they could all year round.

And today was beautiful, made even more so by how William had woken her this morning in his bed. In his arms she felt secure, worshipped and maybe even, a little bit loved? The word *love* reverberated about her skull like a tormenting church bell.

It didn't help that when she tried to ignore what she felt whenever around him, the emotions wouldn't abate. Perhaps she was already doomed and she should just accept what she felt for the man. She sighed. Falling for a gentleman, one who had no plans on staying and had not asked her to marry him was foolery indeed. Not to mention she had promised the mother superior she would see her before the New Year.

A pang of wretchedness swamped her. She'd not

thought to meet a gentleman as loving and caring as William, especially not so close to her departure. And now that she'd sampled the delights that were possible between a man and woman, May was no longer so sure as to her choice.

Footsteps sounded behind her and she looked up, smiling as William sat beside her. His hand ran down her spine and settled atop her bottom. "Behave." She chuckled, not wanting him to behave at all.

He leaned close to whisper in her ear. "You've corrupted me. Behaving in any gentleman-like manner is impossible when I'm around you."

May met his gaze, and the simmering heat behind his jest made her shiver. Only an hour ago they had left each other and yet she wanted him again with a ferocity that scared her.

William's attention shifted to her lips. "Have I ever told you how beautiful your mouth is?" He traced her bottom lip with his finger, running it over her chin before he dropped his hand to his side. "What am I to do with you?"

She checked the whereabouts of her brother and then turned back to William. "I can think of a lot of things."

"You know that's not what I mean." He threw her a pointed stare. "We need to talk about what's happening between us. What this means for both our futures."

May stood and started to dust off her gown. "We don't need to talk about what's happened, and I certainly don't want you to feel obligated to marry me just because I shared your bed. After Christmas, our lives will be vastly different and already planned out. There is nothing to discuss." She called out to Matthew and gestured for him to come back to her. The silence from William didn't bode well and it took all of her strength not to look at him. He didn't move, but she could feel the hardened, angry gaze against the side of her cheek. "I like you William, very much in fact, but what has passed between us and what may happen is unlikely to transform into a lifelong love affair, which I'm sure you would agree."

He stood, towering over her and making her feel small, not an easy feat since she was tall herself. "And I fear you'll live to regret such a choice."

May watched him walk away just as her brother joined her. She frowned, the pit of her stomach churning as to what to do, what she felt and what she wanted in life. Did she really wish to be cosseted in a convent for the rest of her days. To never experience the ecstasy that she'd enjoyed in William's arms. Not really in all honestly, but then, she'd given the mother superior her promise, had assured the woman on numerous occasions her choice was adamant and immovable.

"Is Lord William well, May? He seems a little put out."

She smiled to dispel her sibling's fear. "I think he's going to miss our beautiful home when he leaves, that is all. As will I."

"I don't want you to go." Her brother's bottom lip wobbled and she hugged him to her side. "I'll be all alone as will you. Please stay. Please," he begged.

"When you're older you'll understand why I went, darling. Your future means the world to me and I want you to succeed. I want you to want for nothing and therefore I must go. It's for the best. Trust me," she said, clearing her throat to clear the lump lodged there.

A tear slipped down his cheek and her heart crumbled into dust. She hated upsetting her brother. If only he were a little older he would understand. "There are always other choices and better ones people can make. I know

I'm only young, and you may think I don't understand, but I do. You're doing this for me and I don't want you to." He ran off and left her on the beach staring after him.

May sniffed and sat back down on the sand, hating the fact she'd now upset two people she cared about. *Blast it.*

߷

William strode into Lord Levinstone's office and shut the door behind him with a bang. His lordship looked up from the paperwork, his face a mask of surprise at his sudden appearance. "Forgive me, my lord, but I was hoping I could have a private word with you. It's in regards to your land and your daughter."

Lord Levinstone nodded and placed down his quill. William cleared his throat, his courage failing him for a moment.

"I'm sure you're aware, and I have it on good authority my father notified you before his passing, that I work for the Crown. For some months now, we've been patrolling the southern coastline of England for a sloop, painted as black as the night's sky that's been seen docking not far from your estate."

Not a flicker of reaction passed from his lordships visage and William wondered at it. Surely the populace knew of the ship and its hankering for the area. "I followed your daughter some nights past. It was a moonlit night and she was walking toward the shore. I wasn't fast enough pulling on my boots and by the time I made it outside she'd disappeared."

"This is all very interesting, Lord William, but please hurry it up. Luncheon will be called directly and I need to discuss with the staff what table decorations I wish for Christmas day before I break my fast."

William took a calming breath, annoyance taking hold at that indifferent, aloof tone of his lordship. "I would like to know if your daughter and your family are involved in smuggling. I'm sorry to be so blunt, but you must know it's an offense punishable by imprisonment. Please think on that fact before you answer. I took an oath, my lord."

Lord Levinstone leaned back in his chair, an amused grin forming on his lips. "Well of course we do. Most people hereabouts are middle-class and commoners alike. The taxes are hideous and there are people without the means to afford the most basic of goods. It's not to be borne."

William ran a hand through his hair, not believing the words coming from his lordship's mouth. "Are you telling me you know of and agree to this illegal trade?"

"Well," his lordship stuttered. "It's not really hurting anyone down here in Cornwall, now is it? They only use our caves as storage until the goods are moved on. Not really anything to do with us at all."

"What's in it for you?" William leaned forward hoping the movement would clear his head. It did not. If anything, his mind swam with the thought that the smuggling ring had been right before his eyes this whole time and the one woman who'd captured his heart was one of them. This was the most absurd conversation he'd ever had in his life.

"We take a cut." His lordship became serious. "There is something you must understand before you act on what you've found. Not that you can really do anything as you'll never find contraband in our possession and therefore prosecution would be moot. I have a lot of friends down here, you would be hard pressed indeed to find anyone who'd gainsay me. But," he paused, steepling his fingers beneath his chin, "there is something you must know. Ever since May's mother died, she's taken up the role of protector for me and Matthew. Now, I've tried to dismiss her of this folly, as she's not responsible for either of us. Nevertheless, she continues to worry about the estate and the future of it for her brother. It's why she's becoming a nun, so she'll not be a burden to William in her dotage years. Not to mention her first Season didn't go as planned and she refused to have another. Between us, I do believe my daughter has a preference to becoming an old maid."

"And that's a notion I find ridiculous." William stood and paced before the desk. "Matthew seems to adore his sister, I'm sure he would never see May as a burden." And as for being an old maid, surly after their time together he'd altered her opinion on becoming one of those. "Are you telling me she's a part of this smuggling ring just as a means to keep funds coming into the home? And you allowed such madness?"

"I'm not proud of it, and it's gone on for far too long. May believes leaving us and becoming a nun is her only option. That's why I wrote to you. I need your help."

"My help?" William turned and faced Lord Levin-stone. "What for?"

"I had hoped that if you spent a little time together you may find qualities you liked in my daughter, enough so that you would offer marriage to her."

William halted his steps, turning to face his lordship. "Marriage to a woman who, after hearing what you've just said, I'm now contracted to prosecute." William tried to calm his frantic heart. Images of them together in bed, the emotions she pulled forth from him sent him into a blaze even now. And yet, she was unlawful. A liar.

A smuggler.

Damn it.

He caught sight of her coming back from the beach, her long dark locks blowing in the wind, her gown pulled tight against her legs and showing the most beautiful figure he'd ever had the pleasure of seeing. And it dawned on him like a tsunami of sea water. He was in love with her. A criminal his job was to capture. He shook his head at the ludicrousness of the situation. "The smuggling must stop. If you wish for me to propose marriage to your daughter, such activities must halt immediately."

His lordship tsk tsk'd him, smiling a little as if this was nothing but a lark. "Our agreement is for one last shipment. The smugglers will no longer be docking here due to the fact they've gained some attention, if you understand my meaning."

William knew exactly what he meant. That he and his crew had found them out and the smugglers knew it. "What we've spoken of here today must stay between us. I will confront May in due course. Are we agreed?"

Lord Levinstone nodded. "Agreed. And good luck to you. When it comes to my daughter, I do believe you may need it."

William scoffed and walked from the room. He didn't need good luck. No. What he needed was a miracle. Something told him the strong-willed, independent woman that was May would not be easily swayed to marry him instead of God.

And when she found out about his true reason behind his trip, he doubted she would find that the least forgivable either.

CHAPTER 7

William was avoiding her. Again. May sat nestled on a settee in the library and watched him over the top of her book. He sat at her father's desk, his brow furrowed over the paperwork strewn before him. He hadn't looked at her and had only given a terse good morning when he entered the room this morning. Having not seen him at breakfast she'd wondered why he hadn't broken his fast with her.

May turned back to the book and the first paragraph of which she'd read ten times already and frowned. Was he still angry with her? Their argument of the day before hadn't been so grand. Perhaps he was bored, longed for town life and all the well-versed and cultivated young women he could meet there. A tingle behind her eyelids formed and she bit her lip to stop the onset of tears. What did it matter if he'd lost interest in her? She didn't want a husband anyway. And when she was a nun, she doubted the women at the convent would cause her any angst.

Only problem with all of that was, foolishly she'd fallen

in love with the rogue across from her. Utterly, completely, wholeheartedly in love with him. What a conundrum.

May turned her attention to him a second time, and found him watching her, one finger tapping against his lips in thought. He had lovely lips... sensual, and very, very kissable. Unable to form words she simply stared back. Never before had she ever been tongue-tied, and yet he could make her into a blabbering mess with just one glance. There was something seriously wrong with her if a simple gentleman like William could befuddle her so.

The sound of a carriage rumbling down the drive distracted her and her attention diverted to the windows.

"Your father is heading into town with Matthew. It seems we're all alone."

A shiver wracked her body at the underlying meaning to his words, not to mention the husky tone of his voice that reminded her of their night alone together. Perhaps he wasn't so very tired of her after all. "Is everything all right, William? You seem as if the weight of the world is on your shoulders."

Her attempt at lightening the mood didn't work. Instead, he threw down his quill and leaned back in his chair looking just as serious as before. "Come here."

May placed her book on the floor, and went to join him. Her limbs felt weak at the determination she read in his gaze, although she wasn't sure whether it was sexually driven or from some other emotion. Coming to stand beside him, he reached out and touched her hip, making little circular motions upon her gown.

William rose to his feet, and scooping her up in his arms, placed her on the desk, papers be dammed. His lips brushed hers before skimming across her jaw to the little place beneath her ear that tickled when he kissed it. She clasped his waist and urged him closer still. May could feel his excitement against her leg, and she chuckled as he slid up her gown to pool about her waist.

"You do realize we could be caught at any moment."

Little kisses ran along the edge of her breast and she sighed. "Then we better be quick," he said, pulling back to meet her gaze.

May reached between them and touched him. William sucked in a breath as she opened his front-falls and wrapped her hand about his velvety shaft. To touch him in this way, to feel powerful and seductive at the same time left a heady warm emotion to coil about inside her. Never did she ever think to have a man in her hands so, and to know that with a few well-placed touches or kisses, he was hers to command.

"If you keep doing that I'll not last."

"But you like it, do you not?" May scraped one nail down the velvety skin. "It's so soft and yet rigid. So very rigid." She tightened her grip and stroked.

William groaned. "May—"

"I yearn for you, William."

At her words he took her mouth in a searing kiss. A delicious heat simmered between her thighs, her stomach somersaulting with desire. She ran her fingers into his hair and pulled him close. There was a savage edge to what he was doing with her and oddly she liked it. Made her need for him double in its extreme.

He fumbled with her undergarments, the wooden desk creaking under their weight. William took her quickly, each stroke, deep, measured but perfectly titillating. Her body fought for control, but he gave neither.

William's fingers bit into her hips as he relentlessly gave into their desires. "You're so beautiful. I..."

She kissed him, her body climbing, aching for the pleasure he'd give her before they were finished. "I what?"

He didn't reply just held her tighter, taking her deeper, harder, faster. May shattered within his embrace and letting go of all inhibitions, savored the moment. Tremor after tremor coursed through her veins, and throwing her head back, called his name.

William joined her in her satisfaction, a guttural moan sounded against her neck marking his release.

She smiled, and pulling back, ran a hand over his jaw. A day's growth of stubble rubbed against her palm. His ocean blue eyes held hers with something she thought resembled caution. "Please tell me what you were going to say."

"If I tell you what I was going to say I will not be able to un-say it. And not that I would want to in any case, but I fear your reaction." His voice was low, guarded.

"Please, William."

He scrunched his eyes closed and taking a fortifying breath said, "I love you. I," he paused laying her hand on his heart, "find myself unable to think of anything other than you. Since the moment you confronted me on the beach, hair muddled from the wind, cheeks aflame with anger, I knew I had to have you. Desire, it would seem, has given way to a deeper feeling than I've never felt for anyone else in my life."

Her eyes smarted and she blinked less she become a watering pot before him. William loved her? Relief poured through her like a balm with the knowledge. Thankful she wasn't the only one who was affected by this new emotion. That he loved her was the most beautiful declaration she'd ever heard. May bit her lip, wondering if she should tell him the same and yet, she held the words back. He may love her, but he hadn't asked her to marry him and what would she do if he never proposed. The heart she so willingly gave would be broken forever.

And if William did happen to ask for her hand, would she say yes? Her future was planned; she'd given her promise to the mother superior. To throw a husband into the equation would be troublesome to a degree. She would never fit into London life and all its rules and regulations. She'd already tried town life during her two Seasons, and had failed miserably at it. Too independent, not willing to conform and abide by the rules. Titter like a debutante, nothing between her ears but air. And she didn't want a husband. Did she?

May caught William's gaze and her heart skipped a beat. He'd been patient with their friendship, loving and kind. How could she not want to marry such a genuine man? And yes, marrying William would mean she wouldn't have to become a nun, and surely God would forgive her change of heart just so long as she was happy…

"I love you too," she blurted without thought or regret.

W illiam smiled and pulled her into his arms. "I was starting to wonder if you did or not." He chuckled, kissing her quickly. "You do realize what this means." He disengaged himself from her and settled both their clothing back into place.

"What does it mean?" she asked, a teasing note to her voice.

He sat in the chair and settled her on to his lap. "That you, my darling will have to marry me."

"Really?" Her eyebrows rose and the smile that burst

across her face made the day feel as warm as a summer's eve. "Who says that I shall?"

"I say." He increased his hold, her body fitting perfectly against his chest as if made for one another. "Say you will marry me, May. Allow me to look after you, love you, make a life with you."

"I'm four and twenty. I hardly believe I require looking after, but yes," she said nodding. "'I' will marry you just to be yours."

William kissed her. It only took a moment before it sparked into something hot and full of need, but they couldn't risk such escapades again and so reluctantly, he pulled back. "I will talk to your father tonight and send word to my man of business to draw up the contracts. Never again will you have to smuggle just to save your family, or become a nun. I have more than enough blunt to keep my estate and this beloved one of your family's running until Matthew is of age."

May stiffened in his arms and he realized his mistake. "What do you know of the smuggling?" She wiggled out of his hold and stood.

"Enough." He sighed, cursing himself a fool for mentioning what he knew and now, having to tell her one of the reasons why he was visiting Cornwall in the first place. "I work for the Crown. I'm here visiting your father as he was indeed a close friend of my own, but it is not the only reason. There have been reports of smuggling coming out of this part of the country. I was to investigate and return with my findings. Prosecute all those involved, if possible."

She crossed her arms, looking at him in shock. "Prosecute. Do you mean you intend to place the people involved in jail?"

"Not me personally, but the law will deal with those who've tried to cheat the system." Fear flickered in her eyes before she blinked and it was gone. "I know you're involved, May and I know you have one more shipment to distribute before the next full moon. I cannot allow you to be a part of it."

"You cannot allow me to be a part of it? I'm not your wife yet, my lord. Illegal or not, I have an obligation to Ste —" She frowned. "The smugglers. I will not break my contract so close to its completion."

"Yes, you will. You have no choice." She strode over to the decanter of brandy, poured herself a small glass of the amber liquid and swallowed it in one sitting. William fought the urge to go to her, to promise her protection, if only she did as he wished, what was right after all, but her body language, distant and shielded told him to stay exactly where he sat. "What are you doing?" he asked at length.

"Fortifying myself for the argument we must have." She caught his gaze, her eyes narrowing in temper. "I will make that last shipment to the smugglers, many of whom I've known for as long as I remember. These are my friends and I will not let them down. Furthermore, I do not appreciate the fact you lied to me. Why didn't you tell me who you work for?"

"It wasn't necessary," he answered in a clipped tone. "I do not have to divulge everything about my life to the people I meet. And let us not forget, you were not entirely honest with me either." Her face paled and he hated himself for hurting her. But he'd always been guarded about his position in the government and what he said was true. Had he not found out about the smuggling, he doubted she would ever have told him. To catch thieves one must remain unknown. "I'm sorry to be terse, but that is my decision and you must adhere to the rules."

"You know what you can do with the rules, my lord?" She came over to him and leaned across the desk, her cheeks aflame with the temper he'd only seen the first day he'd met her.

"What?"

"Whatever you damn well please. But know this: I will not be taking your orders now or anytime in the future. Nor will I marry a man who's so pigheaded that he cannot turn a blind eye, just once, for the woman he supposedly loves."

He stood. Honor and love warring within him, and yet, what the smugglers were doing was wrong. He had always been an honest man, and he couldn't allow this trade to go on if he could stop it. "You're asking me to break the law, to break the oath that I took for my King and country. The love I feel for you has nothing to do with these pirates of the sea. You're putting yourself in danger, May. I cannot allow that to continue."

"It is not your choice, William. I've had to sacrifice everything, risk my family, my reputation to keep this estate from sinking under the waves of debt. The smugglers you hate so much have enabled my brother to keep his birthright. I did what was needed, and I will not apologize or change my opinion of this. And I will not change my mind. I'll see you at dinner."

William watched her leave, before she halted at the door, a sprig of mistletoe above her head. A numb emptiness threaded through him and even if he wished to get up and kiss her senseless, he would not. He would give her some time, to think over her words and see the sense to what he said.

"Do not bother asking Papa for my hand. I cannot marry you, my lord." Her voice as lifeless as he felt.

William followed her quickly, caught her at the base of the stairs and pulled her around to face him. "What do you mean you cannot marry me?"

She shrugged out of his hold and moved away. "I don't believe we'll be well-matched. You're too, too," she gestured at his form, her face one of disgust and hurt, "controlling."

Damn it, the last thing he wished for her to feel was hurt. He loved her, wanted her only to see the errors of her way. "I am not controlling. I only want what is best for you. I can remove all your worries if only you'll let me. But I cannot allow you to smuggle any longer. It's against the law. Please, try and understand."

She shook her head, her chin set in a determined line. "I'm not a person who goes back on my word. You're asking me to cheat my friends."

"Yes, so you've said before, although I don't believe 'friends' drag others into such a reprehensible business." A maid exited the dining room with a garland of holly, and slowed her steps as if to listen. William glared at the girl, and she soon shuffled off. "And what am I to you, May?" He leaned in close enough so only she could hear. "Just your bed mate to be used and discarded when you've had your fill? Is your love so fickle that you can love me one moment and not the next?"

A blush rose on her cheeks. "Of course not."

"Then what?" He stepped back. It was clear whatever feelings she had disclosed to him were not as important to her as her loyalty to her thieving, smuggling 'friends'. He ground his teeth, wanting to shake sense into her while all the time knowing it was no use. The suspicious, closed off woman he'd first met on the beach was back, and there would be no reasoning with her. "I wish you well in your endeavors toward a life of prayer. I hope your time in the convent is everything you'd hoped it would be." Sarcasm laced his tone and yet still, she held his gaze with an immovable strength that no matter how many words he said would not shift.

"I'm sure I'll be very happy there." She bobbed a curtsy before leaving him gaping after her at the bottom of the stairs.

William had hoped his less than favorable reminder of her future in the convent may spark some wisdom into her. It had not. William strode out the front door and made his way toward the stable. A good hard ride in the chilly air was what he needed to clear his head. And maybe by tonight May would have thought over her nonsensical words and be ready to rescind her choice.

He scoffed at his own idiocy knowing she would not. And never would.

CHAPTER 8

May watched from her bedroom window two days later as William rowed the small wooden craft out to the large sailing ship where he would disappear from her life, perhaps forever.

A severe ache tortured the area where her heart sat. What had she done? And yet, she knew exactly what she'd done. She'd pushed away the only man she'd ever loved or cared about. How could she have said yes one moment and then throw his offer away without a second thought. Well, she was certainly having second thoughts now, and yet, now it was too late.

The little boat made the larger vessel safely, and she could just make out William as he climbed on deck. He would probably marry another at some time in his life while she would have endless days and nights without color or joviality.

I'm a pigheaded fool.

"Your carriage is here, Miss May."

She picked up her shawl and looked about her

bedroom one last time. After William had stated at dinner two nights past he would be leaving earlier than planned, it seemed the right time for her to leave as well. Being home, a place where she'd fallen in love for the first time in her life, was just too hard to bear. And she could not face a Christmas here, pretending to be happy and merry while all the time sick with regret. Her choice had been simple in the end, and she had written to the mother superior and asked to come early and was granted her wish.

"Thank you," she said, following her maid out of the room.

The house was deathly quiet. Her father and brother both stood at the front doors waiting to farewell her. Threaded holly ran down the staircase and the scent of pine and sea filled the house. From the look of the decorations scattered about the foyer, the house was almost ready for Christmas. A pang of guilt pricked her that she would not be here to celebrate the day with her family, but she pushed it away. This was for the best, it was time she started the new chapter in her life.

Neither of them looked enthused by her choice to go, and she fought the prick of tears. Fear crept up her spine that she may have made a mistake. That the course she had chosen to walk was the wrong one. May sighed, thinking over her last night at home.

As arranged she had met the smugglers and taken into her possession the last shipment of their contraband. She'd returned to the estate just before dawn to a waiting William. Never would she forget the disappointment or the hurt on his face. The imagery of it would haunt her forever.

He'd not said a word, only strolled into the library,

shutting the door in her face, and seemingly closing her out of his life forever.

And she deserved it.

May forced a smile as she came back to the present, and stood before her family. "Well, this is goodbye I suppose, but only for now. Matthew, promise me you'll write and tell me all the news of home."

"Must you go?" her brother whined, taking her hand.

"You know I must, but remember, we'll keep in contact. And you can visit me whenever you wish." His lip wobbled and May pulled him into a hug, the tears so steadfastly held back spilling onto her cheeks. "Don't be upset." She sniffed, kissing his crown. "This is for the best, dearest and in time you'll understand." Her father mumbled something and May caught his gaze. "What is it, Papa?"

"Other than this being the second biggest mistake you've made in your short life, nothing. Nothing is the matter." His voice was gruff, his annoyance almost palatable.

May frowned. "What was my first mistake?"

"William."

Just the mention of William's name sent a longing that threatened to rip her heart from her chest. She missed him and it had only been an hour or so since she'd seen him leave. Not that he'd sought her out to say goodbye. The last two days, they'd been strangers who had no interest in making each other's acquaintance.

"But why can you not stay for Christmas. I don't want you to go."

May kissed her brother and father quickly, unable to listen to anymore of her siblings pleas without breaking down entirely in front of them. "I must go. It's starting to snow."

"Safe travels, my darling daughter. We will write often and visit when allowed." Her father pulled Matthew against his side and waved from the door, disappointment etched on his visage.

May stepped up into the carriage and looked back at them. "As will I. Goodbye."

CHAPTER 9

May leaned into the wind at the bow of Stephen's ship and stared at the endless ocean before her. How she had come to be here made her laugh. Only last week had she commenced her postulancy at The Little Sisters of Jesus, praying, reflecting and giving thanks. And now, now she was free.

Thank goodness, the mother superior didn't know she prayed for a way to leave them, she would've gone to hell for sure. The woman for all her strict rules and beliefs had sensed her unhappiness and asked her to explain her moroseness.

The moment May had sat down to explain, a dam of emotions had spilled out across the mother superior's desk and threatened to drown the poor woman. Surprisingly, the woman had patiently listened and offered her further time to think about her future or to return to her father's estate. May had done the latter and no sooner had she returned home, she had ridden down to the local village and sent out word to Stephen that she needed his assistance and as soon as possible.

She had expected to see him within a month or two at the least, so when he was ushered into the parlor the following day, May knew fate had shown its hand and had confirmed her choice was the right one—William and she were meant to be together.

And now Stephen was chasing down William's ship having been told by another vessel where they were. It was probably not the most intelligent move her lifelong friend had ever made, since a smuggler's ship was always trying to outrun the law, and William was exactly that—the law. But as her friend, and with her promise that William would not take them into custody, he'd agreed to her plan to take her to him. Now she just hoped that her promise could be kept.

"A ship, starboard side, captain," a sailor hollered.

May looked to where the man pointed and could just make out the sails of a ship on the horizon. Orders rained about her and soon their ship was sailing toward the other vessel.

Stephen came to stand beside her. "Are you sure about this, May? Your course in life seemed set."

She smiled. "I know it did and had I not met William, I would've continued to tolerate the life of prayer and service, but I *did* meet him and he's changed everything for me. I love him." She looked at the vessel getting ever closer and excitement along with trepidation thrummed in her veins. Would William acknowledge her? Would he accept her pleas for forgiveness and make her his forever? May did not know, but she supposed, she would soon find.

"Then I'm glad you're chasing what you want. You deserve to be happy." He smiled and the gesture calmed her a little. Everything would work out well.

"Thank you, Stephen. I hope one day you find love as

well. For all your smuggling, you're a good man." And he was the best of men for helping her out in such a way.

৩৯৯

I t took them some hours to chase down the vessel. By now, William's crew had noted their presence and all stood on deck waiting, watching to see what Stephen's ship was doing.

May stood next to Stephen and spied William before he noticed her. When he did, his eyes flared, but no other emotion crossed his features to give her some clue as to what he was thinking.

He would be angry with her. That she could be sure, but she hoped in time he'd forgive her. Not that she could ever submit to rules from him, she wasn't capable of submissive behavior, but if he was willing to be her equal partner in life, *that* she could manage.

"I'm surprised to see your ship and so close to mine. Are you here to hand yourself over to the Crown and right the wrongs you're so guilty of?" William shouted out across the small stretch of water that separated them.

Stephen laughed. "Sorry to disappoint you, Lord Grandison, but I'm only here to return what is yours." He gestured toward her. "Miss May."

William's gaze locked with hers and a simmering heat flared between them. "She is not mine."

May stepped forward and clasped the rail for support. "Can I come aboard and have a moment of your time, my lord?" The crew on both ships hollered and laughed at her request. May glared at each of them and their chortling stopped.

"If you wish it," he replied, crossing his arms, refusing

to offer help in getting her across the short space of water separating them.

Stephen came to her aid and clasped her hand, helping her climb down the ladder to the small boat that would take her to William's ship. She whispered her thanks knowing Stephen would take his leave immediately, giving her the time alone with William.

"Follow me," William barked, the request like an order to one of his men.

May started at his terse words that did little to comfort her. He was angry, but it had been some weeks since she'd seen him. May had hoped he would've missed her as much as she'd missed him and taken her into his arms and declared undying love before all his crew. Followed by hours of making love…

That part of her daydream took place in the privacy of his cabin. But this greeting left her floundering and unsure of his mind-set. Pushing away her fear, she followed him, comforting herself with the thought that should everything go terribly wrong, no matter what William thought of her, he would not hurt her physically.

He led her toward the stairs, taking her below deck. The ship rocked, making her progress awkward. He didn't wait for her, but kept stalking toward his quarters and she followed, taking in as much of the ship as she could.

William had the respect of his crew. For a vessel that was occupied by men, it was clean and shipshape. His quarters were no exception. A large four-poster bed stood hard up against a wall, centered in the large space. A desk with a multitude of charts and papers sat before large bank of windows that looked over the ocean.

May walked toward the window and gazed out over the deep azure sea. With a view like this to wake up to every morning it was no wonder William had never sought to return to his estate with any haste. The door slammed shut and May heard the bolt slide home. She faced him. The muscle at his temple twitched and she wondered if perhaps this wasn't such a well thought out plan after all. Her fingers shook and she clasped her hands before her to stop the nervous gesture from being obvious.

Maybe he'd lied about his position for her. Maybe it was a ruse to get to her smuggling friends. She shook away the unhelpful thoughts and focused on her plan. She was being fancifully absurd.

"What are you doing here, May? Aren't you supposed to be praying like a good little nun?"

His sarcasm stung. "Don't be rude. The sisters at the convent are wonderful people. Just because you don't understand their motives doesn't make their choices any less valid than your own."

He scoffed and sat on the end of his bed. Warmth spread between her thighs at the memory of what they'd done in his bed back at her home. She cleared her throat, needing to think clearly. "We need to talk."

"Really?" His brows rose. "I believe you've already stated what you wished for and felt for me. There is nothing else left to say."

May went to take a step toward him and then thought better of it when he frowned. Determined not to lose him without making him at least hear her out, she said, "I was angry and upset. What I said I wish I was able to take back. I didn't mean a word of it, I promise."

He scoffed. "Thank you for telling me, but it's too late to change your mind. I'm not a man who can tolerate flighty nature in a woman. Nor one who's obstinate to the point of placing herself in danger rather than heeding the advice of others."

She kneeled before him, clasping his hands. "I will never take orders and I'm sorry if that disappoints you, but it was how I was raised. As for the danger you speak of, my smuggling contacts have been my friends since childhood. If it's escaped your notice," she said, throwing him a beseeching look. "I grew up in Cornwall. There aren't too many children about. We don't have a lot of options if we wish to play and have fun."

"I never wanted you to take orders from me, May. I was merely concerned for you. I've met a lot of smugglers since working for the Crown and not all of them are as friendly as you seem to think yours are."

He raised his eyebrows and May sighed. "I should have been more open with you, I know that now and I apologize. And I will never ignore your regard when it comes to my safety again." Regret threatened to keelhaul her. She should have trusted him when he asked her to. Should have trusted in their love more. "Do you think you can forgive me for being so stubborn a criminal even? Will you give me another chance?"

William pushed her hands away, crossing his arms over his chest. "In two days we dock in London. From there I'll arrange your passage back to Cornwall." He stood and left the room. The bolt on the other side of the door slid home, locking her in and ending their conversation. May stared after him, unsure as to what had just happened. But she supposed, by such a reaction, his answer was no. She bit her trembling lip and looked out the windows, the view of the endless ocean going some way in calming her, but not a lot.

W illiam grinned as he paced upon the deck of his ship. His steps light, his mind free from the plaguing worry that had hindered him these past few weeks apart from May—the longest time in his life.

When he'd seen her standing on the deck of the smuggling ship, it had taken all of his strength not to snatch her into his arms and kiss her senseless. Or shoot the bastard who dared stand so close to her person. That he'd made her believe she was returning home was all part of his plan. It wouldn't hurt for her to think all was lost for a little while. His strong-willed May deserved a little set down after her escapades. He laughed and took over the steering of the ship, the pull of the waves and salty cooling wind making the blood in his veins pump to life once more.

Their time apart had seemed endless. Days and nights of continuous torture wondering what she was doing. If she were happy or sad. Regretful even... And now, she was here, with nowhere to go unless he took her. How he loved her and from this day forward, all his adventures would be May's as well. Life was looking promising indeed.

The hours at the helm passed quickly and he sent word to the cook to lock his quarters door after leaving May her nightly meal. For what he had planned with his future wife, he didn't wish for her to escape.

After making his way down to his room, he stood outside the door for a moment listening to the pacing inside. The mumbling and clanging of items confirmed what he'd hoped. May was angry with him. Good. Although the moment he'd seen her, he'd forgiven the little minx.

He opened the door and the sight of her now only

wearing a silk chemise ceased all oxygen into his lungs. Once he'd closed the door behind him, he snipped the bolt and leaned against the wood. "Trying to seduce me now, darling?" William threw his jacket over his desk chair and took his fill of her.

She threw him a mischievous look. "I didn't think it would hurt."

She stared at him with a longing that almost undid his resolve to tease her for a little longer. He ran a finger down her bare arm, her skin exquisitely soft, just begging for his worship. And he would worship her for the rest of his life. "You were never a woman without a plan."

"You have not forgiven me and nor do you want me. I will try anything at this point to win you back."

The dejected tone to her voice pierced his heart and the fight left him. They'd both suffered enough. "The moment I saw you today, I forgave you. And in all the weeks we've been parted from one another, you were all I've thought about." William slipped free the delicate ribbon at the bust of her attire. "And I want you." He clasped her hand, lifting it up for a kiss. "I've missed you."

"And I you." She leaned up and kissed him, her touch tentative as if still unsure of his feelings. He deepened the embrace, pulling her hard against his chest and taking the kiss to exquisite heights that left them both breathless.

William picked her up and walked over to the bed. He placed her onto his quilts and followed her down. She shuddered beneath him as he removed her chemise. Her breasts, a lovely handful, begged for attention, an attention he was only too willing to bestow. Never would he disappoint her again. She moaned as he took the sensitive flesh into his mouth and flicked it with his tongue. Her hips lifted and brushed his aching cock and need thrummed hot and heavy through him. She was so beautiful, such a loving woman and one he couldn't live without.

"If you keep undulating so, I'll be forced to act hastily."

Her fingers scraped along his back and he gasped at the pleasure of it. "I like teasing you. It's enjoyable."

William nipped his way up her neck to lick the lobe of her ear. "You're a minx."

She chuckled and he kissed her. His need spiking when she clasped his length and stroked. Sweat beaded his skin, his body screaming to make her his, for now and always.

He hoisted her leg against his hip, sliding his member along her hot, wet flesh. Unable to stop himself, he teased her nubbin, rocking them both toward climax.

She moaned, begging for more and he would give her more, much more. William clamped down on his resolve and continued to tease, to taunt her flesh. He wanted her to be as desperate as he was, aching and frantic for release.

For so many nights he'd dreamed of seeing her so, of loving her like this if only one more time. The last thing he wished to do was quickly tumble her on his bed and be done with it.

"William, please. Enough," she gasped, her voice husky with need.

He paused his ministrations and held himself at the entrance of her heat. "Impatient are we?" She squirmed, trying to push herself onto him and he chuckled. "I love when you do that," he gasped out as she managed to take his cock head inside her.

"I'm mad for you William. Please, take me," she begged.

Her flushed cheeks and panting breaths told him more than words how excited he made her feel. Intercourse had never been this soul binding before with any of the other women he'd slept with. May somehow managed to make it a new experience once more. Exciting. Torrid. Loving.

He slid into her, his hardened length stretching and filling her with every inch. William groaned and watched as her eyes fluttered shut. He pumped into her, his aim to make their lovemaking last as long as possible. But with every stroke, May matched his desire, clasping him close and driving him to distraction, her kisses demanding, her touch maddening. The sweet sigh of breaths tickling his ear would drive any man to his knees and do her bidding.

William increased his pace, and so too did her urging, before disengaging and flipping her quickly onto her stomach. She let out a squeak of alarm and he chuckled. "Trust me. You'll enjoy this." William kneeled and pulled her to sit on his lap giving him a beautiful view of her stunning back. He pushed her hair to one side and kissed her nape.

"What are you doing?" Her breathless, if not a little shocked question made him smile.

"Trying something new."

May reached behind and touched his cheek. "I'm nervous."

He clasped her hips, lifted her and slowly sank into her wet, hot core from behind. "Relax my sweet, there is nothing to be nervous about." In this position, May controlled the pace and how deep the penetration. At first, she was a little unsure of what to do, but it wasn't long before she gained her rhythm.

William slid his hand down against her patch of curls and stroked her sensitive flesh. Her skin burned, her body smelling sweet, flowery, and good enough to eat. Her breast sat nicely within his other hand, and he reveled in her enjoyment.

His balls tightened at the same moment he felt the first of her convulsions around his member. He stroked her harder, clasping her breast and moaned. William took her until he too found pleasure, his orgasm rolling through him like an endless wave.

May went limp in his arms and he swooped her up, laying her beside him on the bed. He pulled her into the crook of his arm, needing to keep her as close as possible. She watched him in silence and he wondered what she was thinking. If it was anything like his thoughts, they were of marriage, of a future and when they could repeat what they'd just done.

"That was…delightful."

William laughed and pushed a lock of hair over her shoulder revealing the beautiful curve of her neck. "Yes, it was." She sighed and closed her eyes blocking him from the most beautiful view he'd seen for weeks. "Will you marry me, May?"

She smiled but didn't look at him. "Hmm. Maybe."

He laughed at her teasing tone and tickled her a little, enjoying her delight. "I will not let you leave this bed until you agree to be my wife, minx."

May clasped his jaw and ran a finger over his lips. His body hardened even after the enjoyable reunion they'd just shared. "Well, I don't ever want to leave your bed, but I also wish to be your wife. So yes, I'll marry you, but we'll stay here forever too."

William leaned over and kissed her. Hard. Already his body yearned to take her again, to consummate the promise they'd just made. He reined in his desire and pulled back. "Does your father know where you are?"

She smiled. "Of course. He walked me down to the beach to meet Stephen."

He shook his head. May's parent was as devious now as he ever was in his youth it would seem. "I assume that even though we were parted for some weeks, his desire for our marriage still stands?"

"Yes, it does. Before I left he gave me orders to return home married, settled and ready to celebrate Christmas with you by my side. So, I suppose you'll have to take me back to England and gain a special license."

William grinned. "I have a better idea." He sat, picked up his shirt, and then pulled it over his head. "Get dressed and meet me up on deck."

"Why?"

He stopped at the door and turned to see her frantically pinning up her wayward hair as best she could. "There is something I wish for you to see."

❧

The surprise William had wanted to show her was the small island of Guernsey and the town of St. Peter Port where they would dock and marry within hours.

She watched him knowing her visage was a little awestruck. And she was in awe of him and utterly, shamelessly in love as well. In the small amount of time they'd grown to know one another, she'd come to love him unlike any other. It was without doubt she could not and would never live without him again.

A sense of wellbeing came over her, warming her skin and cloaking her in security. William would take care of her and her family should they require it. No longer would she need to worry about expenses or estate costs that had always outnumbered the money coming in from the home farms. All her troubles would be gone with the declaration of marriage from the priest. May wrapped her arms about William's neck and smiled. "I love you. Thank you for asking me to be your wife. Again."

"Thank you for saying yes."

He grinned and her stomach flipped. Yes, she was the luckiest woman on earth and soon they would sail back to Cornwall to have Christmas. The start of a new life, a better life, for all of them.

And one, she couldn't wait to get started.

HER GENTLEMAN PIRATE

HIGH SEAS & HIGH STAKES, BOOK 2

Kidnapped by a smuggling pirate, Miss Arabella Hester is appalled by the circumstances that have befallen her. Imprisoned on a ship in the most scandalous of company, her reputation as a lady betrothed to a English Viscount is in tatters.

. . .

Captain Stephen Doherty aka Blackmore was left with little choice but to kidnap the daughter of Sir Ronald Hester, a man who's payment for services rendered is long overdue. The ransom due on Arabella will settle her father's debt, and allow Stephen to restore his family's fortune.

Pursued across an ocean by those determined to restore a daughter to her rightful place, Arabella and Stephen navigate high seas and high emotions. But when their time is up, it remains to been seen whether this lady wishes to be caught by anyone other than her pirate...

CHAPTER 1

Valletta Harbor, Malta – 1819

"Take her aboard and place her in my cabin. And make sure you tie her up. Tight. She's a bit of a hoyden this one, make no mistake." A deep, rough voice said from behind her.

Lady Arabella Hester, normally a serene woman, growled. A most unladylike sound if ever there was one to be sure, but what was she to do with a dirty piece of cloth tied across her mouth? To be kidnapped was not something she'd ever thought to happen while visiting Malta with her papa, they had many friends, certainly no one that wished them ill, or so she thought...

She shivered as the night air pierced her thin shift, having been pulled from her bed. The lapping sound of water sounded beneath her feet, and Arabella knew she was at the docks. This was a rightful catastrophe!

The captain, bastard extraordinaire grinned and again Arabella was forced into an action beyond reprehensible. She spat on his old, sea-worn boot. He would pay for kidnapping her and possibly ruining her good name should anyone find out. Which no doubt was his aim or worse, to do unthinkable things to her that even she didn't want to face right at this moment.

She tried to squirm free of her captor, standing too close against her back and then, like a sack of potatoes, was flung over the deckhands' shoulders, carried unceremoniously onto the boat, off the main deck and supposedly toward the captain's cabin.

The wooden ships interior oozed with the smell of unwashed men and stale air. Her nose twitched at the rank odor that wafted up from the man carrying her. Did these men have no pride? There was plenty of water about; one would think a wash every few days wouldn't be so hard.

He threw her into a chair and her bottom roared in protest. She tried to rub her sore hide, before he wrenched her hands behind the chair and tied them firmly to the wood.

Arabella fought against the knots, landing at least one solid kick to the captor's shin. He glared at her, but didn't retaliate with violence. "You'll all pay for this absurdity. My father and betrothed will not stand for such foolhardy actions. You will all hang."

Her words only ventured a tighter knot about her ankles. She refused to cringe as the harsh rope bit into her flesh. She glared at the bulk of a man who strode off without a flicker of remorse. The door slammed shut and her imprisonment was complete.

Her eyes burned and she bit her lip to stop the tears from welling and falling over her lids. There wasn't time for emotion. Crying couldn't possibly help her situation. A gun would be handy, yes, but not a blabbering little fool that was threatening to come out and make it's presence known. Arabella took a calming breath and fought to think clearly. Her father would look for her, chase down this pirate and ensure justice, she was sure of it. Her papa, a savvy business man knew everyone who traded on the seas. It would not be long before he found out who'd taken her and rescue her in turn. All she had to do was remain calm and dissuade her captors to do anything beyond forgiving.

She took in the room, which was large for a pirate vessel. Not that she'd ever been on one before to judge. It was also shockingly tidy and clean of dust and grime. It certainly smelt better in here than out in the other part of below decks. A large wooden bed sat against one wall, a desk that if she turned her head a little, could be seen behind her shoulder. Large windows ran the length of the ship's stern. They would give a wonderful view of the ocean should she be able to see out of them, and only *if* she wanted to that was.

Not that she would want to see her island holiday home of Malta disappear over the horizon. At the thought of leaving a place that for the last three months had brought happiness to her and her papa after the passing of her mother, tore pain through her chest. Not to mention society would shun her after this ruination, even the limited London society in which she graced. Her life was just about to start. She was only twenty, it couldn't be over already.

She pulled against her bonds with little luck.

Hurried footsteps sounded coming toward the door and her stomach knotted tighter than those about her ankles. The footsteps paused momentarily at the threshold, before the man she would remember for the rest of her days flung open the door, leaned against the wood and stared at her like a prized jewel.

And that was exactly what she was to him. Coin.

"You'll hang for this, you bastard." The vulgarity of her speech made her pause, but then she couldn't regret it. If ever there was a time for swearing, this was it.

He laughed and slammed the door shut. "I very much hope you're wrong, Miss Arabella." He studied her a moment, his visage one of annoyance and contemplation. "I can call you Arabella, may I not? We are after all going to be spending some time with each other and I do hate standing on ceremony when there is really no need to. I'm Captain Blackmore, but you may call me Stephen."

Arabella narrowed her eyes but refrained from replying. She needed to remain composed, talk herself out of this situation if possible, not annoy the man any more than he already was, having succumbed to such tactics as kidnapping.

"You see, my dear, I perceive no fun to be had at the end of a noose." One side of his lips lifted in a cocky grin and she took a calming breath. "In any case, if you're worried your virginity will be in tatters after I'm through with you, you'll be sadly mistaken. You shall leave this ship in good time, hale and whole. I promise you that." He rubbed his jaw and she noted he had lovely cheekbones for a pirate, before throwing the thought aside. "Your reputation may suffer though I'm afraid... Society can be so fickle, don't you agree?"

A thread of peace flowed through her and his no-nonsense speech. Perhaps there was hope in talking this pirate out of his idea for her. "You need to think about what you're doing and who you're doing it to. And let me assure you, I am a lady and one who has done nothing to deserve this. And do not doubt that just because I am female I do not hold the lofty connections in which to sink this piece of rubble to the bottom of the ocean." Arabella reminded herself she was supposed to be diplomatic, not demonic. "I don't understand why you've chosen me as your victim. I've done nothing to you. I don't even know you." She stated. Perhaps somewhere deep inside this man, there was an honest soul.

He looked down at her over his nose, the gaze mocking. "You may not have done anything to me but someone close to you has. You, Miss Hester, are imperative to my plans. But," he said, coming to stand not far from her, running an idle hand atop his chest of drawers as if to feel the smooth wood. "For now, all you need to know is that these quarters will be your home over the forthcoming weeks and you'll share them with me. Do not try and escape for the only way to do so would be to swim. And I will not be bothered nor do I have the time to fish you out of the ocean should you choose to try your luck. Do you understand?"

She ground her teeth. The urge to tell this kidnapper what he could do with his threats almost overcame her sense of self-preservation. How dare he speak to her in such a way? Then, what was she thinking. Pirates, men who marched to their own illegal drum would never see reason. They only thought of themselves, and not what their actions meant for others. "You can go to hell. To do this to a woman who has in no way injured you makes your heart as black as this ship." And his hair, which was strikingly long as well, and looked wind kissed. Arabella studied his features for a moment, his strong jaw, the severe cut of his cheekbones and blue intelligent eyes spoke of breeding and an affluent lifestyle. He looked as though he belonged in a London ballroom, dancing with the upper-ten-thousand, not here on a ship, kidnapping innocent women as a means to get what he wanted.

He shrugged, walking toward a wooden sideboard and pouring himself a brandy from the decanter. "I'm owed a debt that will be paid. You are worth a lot of blunt, so do be obliging, my dear. I hate conflict."

Arabella fought against her ties to no avail. He watched her for a moment, a laughing light in his eyes, before turning and leaving her alone in the room.

The ship rocked, the ocean lulling her to a false sense of security.

These men were dangerous. Had in fact stolen her in the dead of night from a family friends estate in Valletta. Arabella looked about the room. What was it exactly that had happened to this pirate to ensure such wrath. It certainly wasn't fair to drag her into his financial woes. But again, she'd been told of these men on their boat trip over to Malta, of how they operated and their lack of conscience.

She made one final effort to free herself and then gave up. It was no use and the sting about her wrists only told her to continue the fight would lead to severe scaring. Arabella shut her eyes, her body aching with the need to sleep. Having been bundled into a rough, hessian bag, thrown into a carriage and stowed on a ship's deck had left her near exhausted.

After losing her mama to a wasting disease, they had needed to get away from London. Everything at home had reminded them both of what they'd loved and lost. With the warmth of the Mediterranean sun, each day on Malta had brought Arabella and her papa back to life. She'd become engaged to a man who would elevate their family, and it was a match that would've made her mama happy. Everything had been falling into place.

But no more. Society would shun her family once they found out about her abduction, another blow that her papa could not take. Tears fell onto her shift and she closed her eyes, blocking out the terrible situation she now found herself, but it was no use. No denying of her location could change where she now was.

Muffled sounds from the deck above floated through to her, calls to hoist the main sail, steer toward starboard gradually faded as sleep crept over her.

A welcome respite and one she hoped she would wake from only to find this nightmare was nothing but a figment of her imagination.

I t was not.
Arabella woke with a start as the cabin door slammed against the wall. The pirate captain Blackmore strode in, walked to his dresser and started looking through other articles of clothing.

She blinked and her mouth popped open at the defined, enhancing muscles that accentuated his shoulders and perfect back. His skin was tanned and smooth and dripping with water as if he'd just bathed. From this distance, it looked supple yet flexed with months of tough work aboard a ship's deck.

Illegal work…

He turned and her stomach twisted. The pirate's front was even more defined if that was at all possible. He watched her under heavy eyelids as he pulled on the plain cotton shirt, tying it closed from the chest up. The silly shirt clung to his body and even with him clothed, it did little to hide his form.

Arabella shook herself free from the absurd thoughts running through her mind. Thoughts that included wondering what he looked like without his well-worn breeches on. Was his bottom as toned as his abdomen? Did he wear drawers under his breeches? "You're doing your shirt up wrong. A man of your advanced age should know how to dress himself."

He grinned and looked down at his lopsided tying. "I like doing things that are not *proper*."

The way he accentuated the word *proper* with a look that spoke of endless nights of sin within his arms made her cheeks burn. She scoffed. "Why doesn't that surprise me?" Arabella focused on anything in the room, so long as it was not this wet shirt, heathen before her. He was making her mind addled and as foggy as the moors in winter.

"By the way, to the lady who knows all regarding dressing, but has probably never dressed herself once in her life. I am nine and twenty, so not into my dotage quite yet." He came and sat on the desk, his body looming over hers in the chair.

The smell of ocean wafted from his skin. Surprisingly it wasn't an awful scent although she made a point of gasping for air. "Please move. You smell as rotten as your soul."

"I shouldn't stink at all. I've just bathed which I'm sure you've already surmised. You were after all, quite focused on me as I dressed."

Arabella quickly glanced at him and cursed her foolishness as soon as she did so. She rolled her eyes, knowing too well she'd noticed such things, of how his cheeks were clean-shaven and smooth, his hair recently brushed. She fisted her hands against a scheming pirate she ached to slap. "You should've used soap; water is not enough in your case."

He narrowed his eyes. "And you should know when to speak and when not to. As a reward for your insolent tongue, and the fact you're so well versed in dressing, I'm going to allow you to assist me from now on. When you've learnt to behave and not try to escape of course."

Arabella laughed, the sound dripping with sarcasm. "I will never help you dress and I will never stop trying to get away from you either. No matter what the risk may be to my life. You're a fiend and one who will pay for this folly with *his* life. I promise you that." Not that Arabella knew how she'd accomplish such a thing, but she would try none-the-less.

He shrugged, seemingly unperturbed. "There is no way out of this room unless you like to swim. So I need you to promise me that if I relent and remove your bonds, you will stay where you are and not cause any strife? You're going to be with us for some weeks, Arabella. It would be best if you just accepted the fact you're my prisoner until I deem that no longer necessary."

Arabella glared. "Of course I'll stay here," she said, losing patience. "I don't believe I would enjoy drowning." She paused for breath. "But rest assured, at the first opportune moment, I will be gone."

He grinned. "I do not doubt you will try."

She gasped as he reached around her and slit the ropes free from her hands. His breath whispered against her cheek and shivers raced down her spine. He stood back and once more she could breathe.

He then cut the bonds about her ankles. "You may

thank me now." He stood and looked down at her like an errant child who refused to do as they were told. "You know, for a lady you lack manners."

Arabella growled at his retreating back. Losing control of her temper, she stood, picked up the glass blotter from his desk and threw it at his head. She missed, her aim off by an embarrassingly large amount of feet.

He smiled as she reached for the ink jar, the gesture lighting up his eyes and drawing her in to his deep blue depths to flounder. Why couldn't *something* on the man be awful and ugly?

No. Not Captain Blackmore it would seem.

"Please don't throw any more of my things," he said, grinning. "I'm quite fond of them and I'd hate to have to punish you."

The jar smashed beside his head spilling ink down the wooden walls and splattering a little over his newly worn shirt. Arabella smirked. No one would dictate to her, especially a scoundrel kidnapper. "I do apologize, captain. My hand slipped."

Stephen bolted the door shut and leaned against it. He smiled at Lady Arabella Hester's antics and swearing that continued behind the wooden walls. He had to concede, she was very strong willed. And right now, she hated him. After spilling ink on his last good shirt, he'd promptly tied her back up and threatened again to place a bandana over her mouth. It had quietened her for a minute or so, but that was it.

He headed up to the quarter deck. The day was clear, not a cloud darkened the sky. His men went about their jobs without the need for him to tell them what to do or when to do it. Life was good. His plan had worked and soon the two thousand pounds he was owed would be stowed below decks in lieu of his prisoner.

Stephen went back up on deck and walked toward the wheel, taking over from his helmsman. The wind caught the main sail and their speed increased. The island of Malta was no longer visible and he was thankful of it. The further they travelled from the island the better. Lady Arabella's father would have already dispatched men to save his daughter and her delicate reputation. He needed to make England, London in fact, and fast. It was the only way he'd be able to disappear into the city and keep her safe until the debt owed was paid in full. He had enough friends to keep his location safe, and movable about the city without detection.

"How's the captive?"

Stephen met his helmsman's gaze. "Annoyed. I'd always assumed ladies were of delicate impositions and lightly spoken. This one is an exception to that rule. Her vocabulary, or her preference toward the word *bastard* is enough to make the ladies of her society have an attack of the vapors."

Not to mention how damn beautiful she looked when firing insults against his head. Her brown locks, hanging loose about her shoulders, lips that were plump and just begging for his own to smash against them. Days before he'd kidnapped Arabella, he'd watched her from afar. Her infectious laughter with her friends had often brought a smile to his face. And from a distance he'd noted her height, but even he was shocked to learn her perfect button nose reached his chin. Which brought to mind how long her legs were and since the day he'd thrown her in to his cabin how much he'd enjoy the feel of them wrapped about his waist.

His man chuckled. "You jest." He paused. "In truth Captain, how is she? Do you think she'll try and escape, or cause trouble?"

"I think if she could get her hand on a gun she'd shoot me right dead. But no matter. The little minx will eventually realize she's stuck with us no matter what she tries. Until Sir Hester pays up at least."

Stephen adjusted the wheel and raised his face to the sun. What a fabulous day this was turning out to be. Below his very feet, he had his blunt, feisty as ever and safely stowed in his cabin, while before him, his crew worked hard and were sailing for England.

Not his first choice, Scotland would suit him better, but he'd not had the pleasure to call it his ancestral country home. Thanks to his great-grandfather having lost everything on a turn of a card, or so the old tale went. Time to accept his situation and make the best of his life.

"What will you do if her father refuses to pay you what he owes? We've never killed before and some of the men are raising concerns over your actions, Captain."

Stephen frowned. The last thing he'd wished to do was upset his crew, but after months of broken promises of payment, he'd had to act. He couldn't be seen as weak. All of his crew would be in danger if such a rumor leaked out across the oceans. And it had only taken one look of the chit and he'd known what he would do…

"You have my word I'll not kill her, but I will ruin her should payment not be forthwith. I'll make it well known it was me who'd kept her onboard my ship for months… unchaperoned. By tarnishing her reputation, I diminish her father's good name with it."

His man shuffled his feet looking paler than normal. Stephen's patience faltered.

"Captain, you're not going to rape her? We may be smugglers, pirates perhaps who don't always confirm to the laws of man, but none of us are so unsavory. We have wives, families to care for." He cleared his throat. "None of us wish to swing at the end of a noose for this chit."

"And you will not. That I can promise you. Her father will pay and that will be the end of it."

"I hope so, Captain."

Stephen handed him the wheel and walked about the deck for a time thinking over his men's concerns. Should Sir Hester refuse to pay, his life on the sea would continue for a few more years yet. It wasn't in his plan. The small castle he'd bought and paid for in Scotland required extensive repairs and the funds owed were going to ensure that happened. For the first time in his life, his mother would live in the station to which she should've been born. Not in a fisherman's cottage in Cornwall. His great-grandfather's recklessness with blunt had secured their fate and he'd done all that he could to make his mother's life as comfortable as possible while she waited for him to become a self-made man.

But it wasn't enough. He wanted what was taken from him by no fault of his own. He had gentleman blood in his veins, and god damn it, he'd die with the life of one if it was the last thing he did.

CHAPTER 2

The kidnapping pirate had forgotten about her. For three days he'd left her to wander his cabin, spend every hour enclosed in a space she'd walked around a million times. At least the captain had thought to give her some essentials for her stay. Like a privacy screen, a jug and bowl for bathing and two gowns, even if they were three seasons old, at least they were clean. She'd been able to open a small window to allow the fresh sea air to enter, too small to crawl through unfortunately, but what she really desired was sunlight. And lots of it.

The scrape of her breakfast tray being placed on the floor before her door made her stomach rumble. Today, instead of the ruffian cook she was used to greeting with disdain, this morning the captain himself brought her breakfast.

Good. Maybe she could tip it on his head.

"Your breakfast." He placed it on his desk and stood, legs apart and arms crossed over his chest. A chest barely hidden beneath the half-open shirt he wore. Skin touched by the sun peeked out at her, tempting her to feel the contoured lines that made up his body.

Arabella shook herself from imagining what he'd feel like. She didn't want to touch him, or be anywhere near the pirate if she could help it. "I suppose I should thank you, but I won't. What do you want?"

His lips quirked before he chuckled, showing his straight, lovely teeth. She cursed. "You can thank me in other ways."

"Really, and what do you suggest I do?" Arabella poured herself a cup of tea and took a sip. The beverage went some way in dispelling her bad mood, but not by much. How dare he want thanks from her? She didn't ask to be here, he was holding her captive. It was his duty to keep her from starving.

"After you have broken your fast you're required on deck."

"What?" The tea splashed over her hand and she put the cup down with a clatter. "You're letting me outside? How long are you allowing me this treat? Please tell me it's a day at least."

"That will depend on you. I will see you outside shortly."

Arabella smiled. Sunlight. Oh how she'd missed it and now if she behaved herself she could spend a whole day lazing around on deck enjoying it. She tried to think if she'd seen a chair she could procure while out there so to enjoy the marvelous ocean.

She quickly finished her breakfast, tidied her appearance as best she could considering she was wearing day's old clothing and headed up on deck. When she stepped out into the corridor, Arabella was pleased to note no one stood guard to stop her.

The brightness of the sun after days of being stuck indoors made her squint. Men stopped what they were doing and stared, some looking less savory than others. She glared at them, lifted her nose and walked toward the bow and the magnificent view that opened out before her.

Footsteps sounded behind and she turned. The captain strode toward her. Awareness shivered down her spine at the determined glint she read in his eyes. His hungry gaze raked over her and she swallowed. Hard. "Thank you for letting me on deck." Arabella looked about. "Is there a chair or stool about that I may use for the day?"

His deep rumbling laugh caused her stomach to twist.

"What's so funny?" she asked, annoyed.

"Beside the fact you expect to sit on deck and lounge about while my men work hard for their captain. Nothing at all entertaining about that." The words dripped sarcasm.

"You're not my captain, which I'm sure I need not remind you. You kidnapped me, remember?"

"Aye, I kidnapped you and for good reason, but now you need to work. I don't accept laziness from my crew and that goes for the women whose family is in debited to me. You must work for your upkeep, room and food." He pulled a wooden pole from behind his back with an array of cotton tassels on one end. Arabella frowned at the apparatus having never seen anything similar in her life.

"What is that?" She stepped back, the hard wooden railing pushing against her spine.

"This is a mop and that bucket on the ground over there is what you're going to use to wash my deck. All of it."

Arabella stared at the bucket filled with soapy water. "I will not. I think you're forgetting who I am."

"And who is that?" he asked, an amused grin on his face.

"I'm a lady and ladies do not clean pirate's ships." Arabella's temper rose with the continual laughing expression on his face. She clenched her hand to stop herself from slapping his cheek.

He passed her the so-called mop ignoring her protests entirely. Arabella snatched it out of his hands. "I'm not cleaning your boat."

"It's a ship. And yes, you are."

"Really." She faced the sea then pitched the cleaning apparatus overboard. That she'd denied him the pleasure of seeing her mop his deck like some scullery maid filled her with pride. She turned to him and smiled. "Oh dear, I seem to have dropped it."

He stared at her, his expression seemingly one of surprise and then contemplation. "There is a punishment for disobeying a captain's order." His tone was low, deadly and all amusement vanished from his face.

Arabella's stomach clenched. The word *punishment* didn't sound at all like something she wanted to experience. Did it involve physical abuse? Would he give her to his crew for enjoyment? Would he touch her himself? The thought sent panic spiraling through her limbs making them weak. "What are you going to do to me?"

He called out to one of his deckhands, the man scrambling over as quickly as he could to his captain. "Go to the galley and grab another mop. Miss Hester has misplaced the one kept up here."

"Yes, Captain," the young man said, before hurrying away.

"I dislike you immensely." She took in the size of the ship and the amount of wood she was supposed to clean. It was an impossible duty for her to fulfill and something about the captain's smirk told her he knew exactly what she was thinking. How could he do this to a woman who'd never cleaned in her life. If she did it wrong, which was highly likely, would he make her do it again? It wasn't to be borne.

Not wanting to spike his ire any more today less he throw her back in his room, as soon as the replacement apparatus was handed to her, she set out to finish the job. If by chance this mop went overboard by the end of the cleaning it was not her fault. Accidents happen...

Hours passed, the captain the entire time never far away, watching her every move, the heat of his gaze making her skin prickle more than the sun on her skin. The muscles in her arms burned with overuse and sweat dripped between places sweat should never drip. In no way had she ever been made to work so hard in her life. Should society see her now, hair limp about her face, her dress ruined by grime, her fingers bruised and bleeding, she would never be allowed back in the glittering ballrooms of the *ton*.

Not that that would tax her too much. Society had never drawn her like so many other ladies of her class. There was no adventure, no chance of a grand love just waiting for her across a supper room table. Her life, just as her father wished it to be, was full of order and conformity. And her betrothed was exactly like him. She scrubbed harder against the wood, her life like the ocean before her, a never-ending swirl of boring. Although she had to admit the ocean wasn't always so calm and peaceful.

When she'd met Lord Frederick Montague, a viscount with large holdings in Somerset, for the first time her life seemed complete. He would love her immediately, be gallant and kiss her senseless.

He did not.

Instead, he'd looked at her like she'd sported some beastly bug on her face, sniffed and continued to talk to the gentleman beside him at the dinner table as if she didn't exist. And for the few weeks he'd graced their life in Valletta she hadn't been his priority. Lord Montague had gone about his days making sure to stay well away from her and ensuring no more than a good morning and good night was spoken. To just image her betrothed coming to save her was absurd.

He was ridiculous and there was nothing she could do about it. She scrubbed the deck harder. The contract was signed and her father overjoyed. And as much as Arabella loved her papa and wished to make him happy, something told her the moment she married Lord Montague she would never be so again.

Arabella huffed out a breath. Visiting Malta had had its advantages and her time there had enabled her heart to heal a little after losing her dear mama. Although the society was large enough to house fabulous balls and entertainments during the Season, it also left a lot of time to fill. Over the weeks of their stay she'd become friends with a daughter from a local family who graced the same social sphere. Nina, or Miss Rowsley had often attended the nightly parties with her and helped her sneak out a time or two to mask balls that they were forbidden to attend.

She would miss her friend dearly and she knew who to blame for that.

She stopped to have a break, and her attention was pulled to where the captain stood steering the ship. His muscled arms flexed with their task, his upper body bared to the elements and bronzed by the sun.

The urge to lick her lips like a droplet of him was sitting there fought with her self-control. She didn't like this man any more than she liked her betrothed. Although, she had to admit, at least the captain spoke to her. It was more than Lord Montague had ever done.

She studied him for a moment. Reveled in the power his presence exhibited. A queer flutter took flight in her belly and for the first time in her life, Arabella wondered what it would be like to lay with a man.

The thought pulled an array of others with it. Like how many women *had* he seduced. Did he have a special woman waiting for him somewhere? Did he find Arabella attractive or only a means to an end?

Their gazes locked and her mouth dried. His intense stare sizzled the space separating them and under no circumstance could she shift her attention elsewhere. From the short distance between them he took in her every feature. His inspection left little to the imagination. Heat bloomed up her neck and she turned to look out over the ocean.

He was a rogue through and through and one that with just one look could make her forget who she was and what he'd done to her.

Worse, Arabella had a feeling he could also make her forget the society in which she was born with just one touch.

CHAPTER 3

She was tied up again. Arabella sighed. It seemed throwing the captain's second mop and bucket overboard had pushed the man too far. But never would she allow him to make her do such a menial task again. Her arms still ached, a fact that wasn't helped with them being tied behind her back.

The sun had long gone down and her stomach rumbled, reminding her of the late hour. She was being punished. Dinner had not been forthcoming and the thought of missing out brought tears to her eyes. Would he feed her at all tonight?

Gosh she hoped so.

She glanced over his desk and spied the apple sitting on a tray. Not being able to reach for it made her stomach cramp even more. The captain would pay for this abuse.

Wiggling her bonds was of little use and so she sat and waited for when he decided to turn up. If ever. Laughter and loud jests sounded from the deck above. Someone played a pipe instrument of some sort that made these sea fearing men dance, if the loud steps were anything to go by.

It was obvious that in their enjoyment they'd forgotten about her. Were content to let her starve to death.

The door opened and she almost sighed in relief, but the severe set of the captain's face soon stopped all mirth. His eyes were sleepy, a day's growth of beard marked his strong jaw. Arabella swallowed the trepidation that took flight in her gut. He was foxed. Her attention snapped to his bared torso and the corded muscles that flexed with each breath.

She should look away with disdain. She was a lady, a woman of impeccable breeding. How dare he make her want to take that final step on her discoveries of men and have him show her all there was to experience. That was what her betrothed was for.

Arabella's mouth gaped as her gaze followed the taut V of muscle that disappeared into his breeches. She started at her own thoughts, which were anything but innocent. One night when she and Nina had snuck out, they had heard music while passing the mews. They stopped and spied on the servants and what they'd seen there had opened her eyes to what men and women did when alone. Of what the male body looked like in the throes of passion.

She bit her bottom lip, imagining exactly what this captain would look like in such a position.

Arabella started at her own thoughts. What was she doing thinking in such a way? This man had kidnapped her. Made her work like a servant. Forgot to feed her. He'd be lucky if she didn't spit in his face. "I do believe you've forgotten something."

He raised his brow and contemplated her with a glance

that she didn't even want to surmise over. "What would that be?"

His deep baritone, slightly slurred with liqueur had an odd twang to it. Similar to those who hailed from Scotland. Arabella frowned. Where was he from before sailing the high seas?

"My dinner. If you haven't noticed in your drunken state, it's near the middle of the night and I'm starving. Now turn about and go fetch me some." He laughed. A great holler that irked even more than being starved. He found this amusing? "I'm not joking, Captain Blackmore."

He rubbed his eyes and beckoned to a man she hadn't seen standing behind him in the shadows. Her mouth watered as the smell of chicken broth and a plate of vegetables and bread was placed before her. Never had food been all-consuming and never had she been more desperate to eat it.

The lout didn't move to release her bonds. Was he planning on teasing her with the meal all night? The thought of such punishment almost brought tears to her eyes. "Unless you're going to feed me yourself, you had better untie me."

"Interesting concept and one I'm only too willing to try." He pulled up a chair before her and picked up the bread. The dough smelt newly cooked and delicious. He tore a little bit off and held it before her lips. Arabella met his gaze over the top of his fingers. It wasn't just food he was offering, but a taste of sin. Something told her, should she take a bite, her life would never be the same.

Her heart pounded as she leaned forward and took the food from his fingers.

❧❦❧

S tephen inwardly groaned as her sweet lips opened and she took the piece of bread into her mouth. Thoughts of other things going into the orifice bombarded his mind and his cock twitched. He'd planned on staying away. Of letting her starve for one night.

The woman was trouble and more annoying than he thought she was going to be. The fact she had thrown two mops and a bucket overboard irritated and amused him at the same time. Who did that type of tomfoolery?

He hadn't expected it from a woman of her breeding and yet he liked her spirit.

From all reports, she should be frightened of him. Submissive and demure. Instead, he'd been dealt a harridan who hadn't reached old age. She chewed and closed her eyes, seemingly enjoying the repast. A twinge of guilt pricked his conscience. He'd never been one to starve anyone, least of all a woman, but there was something about this minx that rubbed him the wrong way. Or worse, rubbed him entirely the right way.

He cleared his throat. "Better?"

Her glistening, deep green eyes met his and for a moment he lost himself in their depths. She was an exquisite woman. Her body was one he could spend hours devoted to. A nice pair of breasts he'd watched longingly all day, long, lean legs that would wrap nicely about his waist and beautiful brown locks that cascaded over her delicate shoulders.

"Please tell me you're going to give me more than a sliver of bread."

He grinned at her gumption. What a remarkable spirit. He doubted anyone could break her, and he hoped no one ever did. She was magnificent.

Stephen ladled some soup onto the spoon and held it against her lips. She moaned as the liquid hit her tongue. The intoxicating sound made him fumble with the cutlery. Desire coursed through him and he adjusted his seat knowing if he made it through the meal without ravishing her, it would be a miracle.

His captive ate every bite of her repast. He leaned back in his chair and watched her. She didn't say anything, no thanks or comments on the meal, just held his gaze with a forthrightness he'd never experienced before. Not with a woman at least.

"You're not scared of me, are you?" he asked at length already knowing what the answer would be.

She scoffed. "Why would I be? I'm worth more to you alive than dead. And since I figure we're headed for London I assume you intend to return me to my family when you've been paid your *supposed* debt."

"Not supposed," he said, interrupting her. "Owed."

"In any case, I'm sure Father and you can come to some sort of agreement without my reputation being sullied."

Stephen nodded. "I'm sure we can." He poured some wine before untying her. She grabbed the goblet and drank deep. He really shouldn't have left her for so long. "Tell me, should you escape this kidnapping reputation in tack, just what are the plans for the determined Miss Hester?" Sadness flickered through her gaze and he wondered at it.

"I'm betrothed. In only a few weeks, I'll be Lady Montague. A countess no less. The marriage is set to take place at his country estate in Shropshire. I consider myself very fortunate to marry a man of good breeding and upstanding values. Some of which are noticeably missing on this boat." Her perfect nose rose in the air with her speech.

"Ship." He smiled at her barb. He should call her Cat. Her claws were sharp enough. "You wound me." He placed his hand across his chest for emphasis. "Do you believe marriage will make you happy? Will the esteemed Lord Montague make you happy?" Stephen started, wondering why he'd ever want to know the answer to such a question. Miss Hester meant nothing to him.

She frowned, small lines appearing between her brows. Instinctively, Stephen reached out and caressed her frown lines away. Touching her like this, without them having argued first sent liquid heat pouring through his veins. The soft flesh did strange things to his innards, made them tighten with need.

"I hope he will."

Stephen hardly heard the whispered words. He traced her perfectly arched brow before letting his hand drop to his side. Not a freckle spotted her nose, not a blemish anywhere. A true English beauty if ever he'd beheld one. "And if he doesn't?"

Somehow he'd leaned closer. Close enough for her breath to whisper against his cheek. He ran his hand down her neck and across her shoulder, her increased breathing making her breasts push against her gown. He clenched his jaw as desire rushed through him.

She shivered. "There is nothing I can do about it in any case. I will have to be content with what I have."

Content? The delectable Miss Hester deserved much more than content. Her life should be full of passion, adventure, life. No matter what his dealings with her father, she deserved much more than mediocre. He wanted to touch her more, to run his hand across her breast and seduce her to sin. Stephen gritted his teeth and pulled back. Fought with what little there was left of him as a gentleman and not act a cad. "If ever you decide to see what life could be like with a real man, just ask me. I'm more than willing to show you."

The words left his mouth before he could stop them. Around this woman, he lost all sense of control and decorum. Her eyes flared before a blush stole over her cheeks. "I'm sure that won't be necessary. In any case, do you not have a woman at some port, just lying about waiting for her pirate captain to ravish her?"

"Ravish? You do hold me in high regard." Sarcasm laced his tone. He liked a good tumble as well as any other, but he never ravished women. Where was the fun in that? Should a woman lay with him, he liked to receive as well as give pleasure. There was nothing he wanted more than a willing participant in bed sport. "Perhaps you ought to have a taste of my abilities. I promise I won't bite. Much."

For the first time he pulled a grin from her lips and it dazzled him silent. He hadn't thought Miss Hester could get any more handsome. How wrong was he?

"Thank you, but no. I'm sure my future husband will do quite well enough. And you never answered my question."

"What question was that?" He crossed his arms over his chest and leaned back in his chair. The thought of Lord Montague doing any woman justice in bed laughable. From what he'd heard of the fortune hunting popinjay, his tastes leaned more toward his own sex than those of the female kind.

"Is there a special woman in your life? Are you married or have you been?" Was that a tinge of interest in her query?

"You do ask a lot of questions for a captive woman. Why would you think I would answer them in the first place?" Stephen asked, enjoying the banter between them. For the first time since he'd thrown her delectable derriere over his shoulder, she was speaking to him in a relative normal manner.

"I suppose you don't have to. I was just curious about your life. It's a trait my father has tried to cure me of, but with little success. I am what I am."

Stephen caressed a curl that had fallen over her shoulder. Never in his life had he wanted to kiss a woman so much. She watched him, the question in her eyes asking if he would act on his desires or not. "There is nothing wrong with who you are."

"I don't believe you know me well enough to make such a claim." She pushed his hand away. "Now, if you don't mind I'd like to go to bed."

Stephen stood and held out his hand to assist her up. She stared at him a moment before allowing him to help. Her fingers were cool to the touch and so much smaller than his. "I think it's time for you to commence the task I asked of you when you first arrived."

"What task was that?" She stopped near the bed just as she reached for the covers.

"To help me dress and undress. I require your assistance morning and night." He grinned at the disdain that bled into her features.

"The hell I will. Undress yourself and somewhere else. You're not sleeping in here."

He walked over to her and tipped up her chin. Her lips opened on a gasp or invitation he wasn't sure. And as much as he wanted to take her, taste the sweet essence she possessed, he refrained. "Come, Miss Hester. Surely you do not wish to be tied up again until you succumb to my demand."

The look on her face said more than any words could just what he could do with his demand. What a minx. A refreshing, feisty chit. He could get used to having her about.

She huffed out a breath of annoyance and reached for the buttons on his breeches. "Let me get a couple of things clear before I do this. Under no circumstance do I wish you to think I'm enjoying myself in the least, because I'm not. This is a vile, un-gentlemanly thing to make a woman do under the circumstances."

The first button popped and he swallowed. His body yearned for her. Right at this moment, it wasn't beneath him to beg for just one touch.

"Secondly, should I find out you've gone crowing on deck that you've made your captive demean herself so, I will cut off the appendage you're so determined for me to see and when you least expect it. Do you understand?" Her voice was authoritative, and damn well near undid him. He loved a woman with courage.

"I understand entirely," he said on a gasp when she accidentally grazed said appendage.

She ripped the buttons clear apart. "Very good then. We're in agreement."

ॐ

The bravado Arabella fought hard to show was exactly that. A show. In no way was she un-rattled by what the captain was making her do. Her fingers trembled as she slipped his breeches over his bottom and down his thighs. She let out a breath when she noted the lack of drawers under his pants.

Worse was the fact she allowed her hand to touch his skin, reveling in the warmth and smoothness begging to be stroked.

She had to bend before him to take them to his feet and she would swear she heard him groan. She wasn't fool enough not to know he was enjoying himself. He probably wished she would touch him, tease him into seducing her.

Never. There was no chance of that happening, in this lifetime or the next. He may be the most handsome pirate she'd ever seen and possibly the nicest one, other than the tying up and forgetfulness with food, but that didn't change what he'd done to her.

"There, you're naked. Are you happy now?" She raised her brow and tried not to notice the jutting member of his body that demanded attention. Arabella stood, hating the fact that once again the captain smelled of the sea, with a hint of brandy. His hands clenched at his side and she tore her gaze away from his body to look him in the eye. "Well?" she asked at length when he didn't reply.

"You're determined to ignore me, aren't you?" He stroked himself and Arabella didn't know where to look or what to do.

She walked around him not wanting him to see her mouth agape like a fish. She fiddled with the bed sheets. "Determined? I thought I *was* ignoring you." Sitting on the bed, she removed her slippers and slid off her stockings. It was so lovely not having shoes on after so many days, but what she'd really love was a bath. A nice, deep, fragrant bath.

Laying on the bed, she turned away and set herself to going to sleep. It was little use. As soon as she closed her eyes, images of his form bombarded her mind. Long, muscular thighs. An abdomen she could use to wash clothing on. Eyes that were sleepy with sin and need. His member…

Arabella's stomach clenched. She shouldn't even be thinking of him in those terms. Her body was becoming a traitor. The captain was a criminal, and awful blot on society that no woman of her class would ever look at or give themselves to. Maybe the trauma of being kidnapped had damaged her mind and principles in some way.

The bed dipped and her tension spiked. Whether in fear or trepidation she wasn't sure. Without another word the captain settled into the bedding, seemingly content to sleep without molesting her. It was a ridiculous situation. Making out one was asleep when you knew the other was not was absurd.

She peeked at him through her lashes. He was lying on his back, one arm acting as a pillow beneath his head. He stared at the ceiling, his face relaxed but contemplative. What was he thinking? Was he hoping she'd crawl up over his chest and kiss him? Slide her hand along his smooth stomach until she hit the apex between his thighs and stroked him harder than he already was. Heat pooled at her core and she inwardly cursed herself to Hades.

"Goodnight, Arabella."

The air in her lungs vanished. Her name on his lips wasn't anything she wished to hear now or ever. It rolled off his tongue in the brogue she'd heard only once before, eliciting a deep-rooted sense of rightness to spark in her soul.

Damn the man. "Go to hell," she replied, rolling over once more and giving him the view of her back.

Her conflicting emotions were absurd as the situation

she now found herself. Arabella clutched the pillow, refusing her body to turn back to the captain and take what he offered. A night of passion, most likely the only one she'd ever enjoy, but she could not. He had wronged her, taken her against her will, damn it. In Malta her life had been organized, planned, her future set and no matter how droll it would be, it was her lot in life. She could not go to her marriage bed ruined.

Despair washed over her like a wave. Who was she kidding. She was already ruined thanks to the ass beside her. Damn him.

CHAPTER 4

A rabella woke in a tangle of arms and legs. A solid heartbeat thumped beneath her cheek and she stilled as realization hit her. She could not be asleep, cuddled up to the most inappropriate man she'd ever met in her entire life.

His hand slid down her back and she inwardly cursed. The shift she'd worn to bed had twisted about her waist and she couldn't move. She tried to ease away, not wanting him to find her in his arms like some wanton hussy he picked up in a port.

"Going somewhere?" His voice sounded husky with sleep.

Arabella jumped and met his gaze. "I think it's obvious that I am." She scrambled back, but not quick enough. He rolled her onto her back, his lower body tantalizingly close to the apex of her thighs. Again, heat pooled at her core and she fought not to let her legs open to him and show him without words what her body desperately craved.

The touch of a man. Not a boy who ignored her, enjoyed his friends more than his betrothed, but a man who enjoyed women, pleasured them and left them wanting more.

As if sensing her need he pushed gently against her. Arabella gasped and fought not to give way to him. He no longer looked sleepy but intense. His whole being zeroed in on her, waiting, wanting, asking a silent question she could not answer.

Not because she didn't want to but because her voice seemed incapable of function. She cleared her throat. "Get off, you brute."

He did as she asked, grinning before he sat up on his elbow. The sheet dipped past his stomach and again she was reminded of his spectacular form. He patted the bed. "I was enjoying our closer arrangement. Perhaps you'd like to remove your shift and come and join me again."

Arabella clenched her fists. He was impossible. *Impossible to ignore...* "I think somewhere along our association you've become confused. I don't want to have anything to do with you. I just want you to get whatever you think is owed so I can leave. This is all."

"Did you know that when you slept in my arms, you stroked my chest and sighed? I think deep down in your conscience you want me." *Could he sound more smug?* He flipped the bedding back and stood, giving her the first full view of his back.

Oh, good God. It was perhaps just as perfect as his front. She shook her head as he stretched, even at this distance, his strength and height making her feel minuscule in the room.

"That's it. I've had enough." Arabella pulled at her skirts that were caught beneath her bottom; fell onto the floor trying to get as far away as possible from him that she could. She scrambled to her feet, stormed over to his armoire and pulled out a shirt and breeches. Walking up to him she threw them at his face. "I demand you clothe yourself immediately."

"Not without the help of my new valet."

A lock of hair slipped over his brow as he drew the clothing away from his face. He was a fiend of the worst kind. She had to give it to him, he really was trying to annoy her to the point of despair. Arabella laughed despite herself. "You're impossible."

He pulled the shirt on himself and grinned. "And you, miss, look delightful when you laugh. You should do it more often. It may delay the effects of becoming an ape leader before your time."

She gasped as he strode out the room, naked from the waist down and without a care to the fact. He was an enigma and one she doubted she would ever understand.

A rabella paced the small chamber, the temper boiling inside her hotter than the Italian sun. For two days she'd been locked up in the room with minimal interaction with people. At this moment in time, she'd gladly talk to the lowest deckhand if only to hear someone else's voice.

She slumped onto a chair. Why had she been left alone again. They had parted on reasonable terms. Other than her being called a future ape leader, but then she really couldn't see the insult in that. There were worst things.

Over the last few days she had thought about putting her circumstances aside, and forming a truce. She couldn't stay indoors forever. Just a day was enough to put her into a decline. It couldn't go on.

The door opened and four men entered. Arabella clutched the desk chair she was sitting on not fully comprehending why they were there until they pulled a tub through the door and placed it to one the side of the room. Over the next few minutes, other men brought in buckets of steaming water.

A bath. There was a god.

"Forgive me for leaving you to your own devices for the last two days. I was required on deck." The captain walked over to a shelf and grabbed what she assumed to be soap. "You may bathe in privacy. Come outside when you're done. I wish to wash also. You'll find clean clothes that may possibly fit you in the chest of drawers, although you'll have to be content with men's clothing. It's all I have."

Arabella nodded. "Thank you. I can't tell you enough how much I want a bath." Just the thought of that warm soapy water made her want to strip down to nothing right now. Captain present or not.

No sooner had he arrived he was gone again. She undressed quickly and moaned as she slid into the fresh, hot water. She washed herself thoroughly, scrubbed her hair and then laid back to soak for a few minutes. Days of grime became nothing but a memory as the water cleaned away her immediate troubles.

Should she die right now she'd die happy.

⚜

Stephen looked over to his cabin door once more and still Arabella wasn't to be seen. It had been well half an hour since he'd left her to bathe. Surely, the woman wouldn't still be in there.

The thought of the soapy water cleansing her skin made him ache. He ran a hand through his hair before turning about and heading toward his room. Maybe she'd fallen asleep. Drowned even. Was right at this moment dead. He quickened his pace, and without heed he threw open the cabin door and stopped.

His imagination had nothing on what Arabella looked like, naked, dripping with water and smelling of lavender. She squealed and pulled the small drying towel about her, but it didn't matter. The image of her long legs, perfectly sculptured waist and breasts that would fit his hands nicely burned permanently into his mind.

"What do you think you're doing? Get out."

A blush stole up her neck making her cheeks very pink. "You were taking so long. I thought you may have fallen asleep and drowned."

She rolled her eyes. "I'm not a child. Don't be absurd."

"I can see that," he stated, allowing his gaze to slide over her again. His jaw clenched. Shutting the door behind him, he leaned against the wood. Hoped that in some minuscule way it would keep him from striding over to her and kissing her senseless.

Her eyes narrowed. "You shouldn't be staring at me like that and you shouldn't be in this room. You need to leave so I can dress."

Stephen grunted. He supposed he should do everything she asked, but he could not. "If I do as you ask I want a favor in return."

"What sort of favor?" She stepped back, wariness settling in her eyes, but Stephen could also see curiosity mingled within her dark green orbs.

"Come here." His command surprisingly worked. Each step she took swayed her hips in a silent seduction. As she stood before him, he ran his gaze over her delicate features. She was exquisite and not someone who should be wasted on Lord Montague. That man couldn't appreciate the woman's form if she was laid out before him on a salver.

He ran a finger down her arm and tiny goosebumps rose on her skin. "Have you ever been kissed?"

She didn't reply, only shook her head.

"Then let me remedy that immediately." Stephen leaned down, cupped her jaw and claimed her lips. Kissed her with all the pent up passion, desire, and respect he could summon.

Her lips were soft and he couldn't help but notice untutored. He supped from them, beckoned her to copy, to follow his lead. And just as quick as her wit, Arabella kissed him back. He groaned as her fingers spiked into his hair, pulling him close. Fire coursed through his blood and he walked her backwards before pushing her up against the door.

Her mouth opened on a whimper and without thought, he took advantage and deepened the embrace. She tasted of wine and smelt of flowers. An intoxicating mix if ever there was one. The glide of their mouths, wet and wanton made him burn. With a will of their own, his hands ventured from her jaw to travel down her waist.

Arabella wrapped her arms about his neck and took control of the kiss. For a moment, Stephen lost all thought as her towel slipped to the floor. He grappled with the fact she was naked in his arms, and seemingly oblivious to what had happened to her only piece of modesty. For a woman who was new to the art of kissing, she was doing a wonderful job.

Her breasts pushed against his chest, her nipples hard little beads that begged to be kissed. There was no doubt where this kiss was leading, and Stephen wanted to conclude this little interlude with his cock buried deep in her willing core. He clasped the perfect mounds of her ass and the action shocked the little minx to her senses. *Clever lass.* Had she kept kissing him the way she was he would've seen just how far she would've taken the interlude.

She squeaked, her eyes darting down to her naked form before she pushed at his chest. With reluctance, he pulled back, giving her the space she wanted. Her emerald eyes sparkled with desire and now unfortunately, loathing. His gut clenched. Touché, Arabella for he too wanted her more than he'd wanted any other woman before, and yet his loathing was not the same as hers.

He loathed the fact she was the daughter of a man who had wronged him. Loathed that his grandfather, his excess in the gambling hells had made it impossible for Stephen to court her as an equal, as it should have been.

"Excuse me." She walked over to his cupboard and pulled out some clothes. Without a flicker of embarrassment, she dressed before him. Stephen stood rooted on the spot, his mouth gaped and his body ached with longing and denial. Of all things holy he wanted her.

He also knew when to stay away. She walked out and slammed the door behind her. She was angry with him and with herself, he could guess. He ran his hands through his hair. He shouldn't have kissed her. She wasn't here to become his chère-amie no matter how much he wanted the fact.

Needing to distract himself, he quickly stripped and jumped into the tepid bath water. It didn't help him. If anything, the aroma wafting up only pulled him further into the delectable lady's lures.

He ran a hand over his jaw and scratched the stubble there. He wanted to have her, that was a given. But this endless longing to hold her, tease her, talk to the chit was beyond his normal reactions when around a beautiful woman.

So why was it so different with Arabella?

The fact she hated him, wanted nothing to do with him and certainly had no desire to bed him couldn't possibly be the reason. Although after their last interaction, the latter may not be so true. Did she desire him as well? The thought jumbled in his mind and even Stephen had a hard time disbelieving it.

Someone so unattainable, above him, beyond his social sphere shouldn't be someone he wanted so much.

But he did. Desperately.

He found Arabella at the bow looking out at the setting sun. The light altered the color of her hair and sent strands of fire flicking throughout the dark brown locks. "You may dine on the deck with me and my crew tonight."

She didn't acknowledge him; just continued to stare straight ahead. "You can't kiss me like that again." Arabella turned and pinned him with her determined gaze. "I'm betrothed. You're a kidnapping pirate. You cannot go about kissing women you're only too happy to steal away and ruin. I won't allow it."

The mention of her future husband made his gut churn like he'd eaten rotten fish. "Are you in any way acquainted with Lord Montague? Or was this just another absurd notion of your father's?"

"Don't mention my father to me. You're already reprehensible, don't make yourself irredeemable," she said, her voice thrumming with anger.

Stephen stepped before her and clasped her arm, stopping her from escaping. "Does that mean you think me redeemable?" He grinned at her ferocious glare. "That the impeccable Miss Hester could possibly look past my misdemeanors and see the man inside." Stephen started at his own words. Did he even want her to see the real him? And if she did, what was he willing to do about that.

Arabella burst out laughing and he raised his brow. He thought over what he'd said and couldn't see anything amusing in it whatsoever. "Are you finished?" he asked at length, when tears threatened to spill down her cheeks.

"The man inside? You'll be sprouting poetry next, Captain Blackmore." She poked him in the chest and his body reveled in the contact. Little as it was. "I will never see you as anything other than a lying, stealing rogue. I should think you made the decision to be who you are many years ago, and set out quite determinedly to accomplish it. And since being here this last week or so, I see nothing but amusement and enjoyment with how your life has played out. There is no underlying man inside. Only an ass."

Stephen swallowed the bile that rose in his throat. The venom in which she'd spoken only proved that she believed every word she said. Yes, he'd had to choose a certain way of life, and maybe it wasn't what he should've been born to do, but it was the only option open to him. The fact that her father now owed him funds that were imperative to secure his and his men's future only coiled the anger inside him tighter.

He was asset rich, but coin poor and the repairs required to his estate were substantial. Once his life on the high seas was over, he'd planned on living in Scotland and enjoying the rest of his days in peace and above the law. Arabella's father and his lack of payment had already delayed him by a year. Everything cost something, and it was about time Lord Hester came to realize that fact.

He gritted his teeth. "Well, my dear. I look forward to proving you wrong."

She patted his chest, the gesture patronizing. "Don't tax yourself. It's not possible." She walked over to the makeshift table on which dinner was being laid out and sat.

He would look forward to the challenge.

CHAPTER 5

Arabella spooned up the fish soup, a soup that would've tasted nice should it not contain fish. She tried to hide her shudder of revulsion and failed. How people could live months on end, day after day of this type of diet baffled her.

The stars were out this fine night, not a cloud to be seen and it was as if she could reach out and hand and pick one from the sky. The water lapped at the ship's side as it forced its way through the waves. It was truly beautiful. She adjusted her seat and enjoyed the freedom of movement her breeches afforded her. How wonderful it must be for men, to be able to wear such clothing always.

But it was all a rouse, for sitting at their table was their captive. A woman here against her will and they all knew it. Picking up a dried piece of bread, she broke it in two and took a bite, watching the captain as he spoke to his crew at the opposite end.

His hair was ruffled, his shirt partly open and exposing the light dusting of hair that feathered his chest. One arm lay lazily before him on the table, while the other was slumped over the back of his chair. She shook her head. It wasn't a pose she was used to seeing at table. No one ever sat so relaxed, certainly not in her world. The captain threw back his head and laughed and Arabella had to admit, she enjoyed this ease of speech and meal more than the one she grew up having.

She turned to the man sitting beside her. "How long will it be before we make England?"

He choked on his brew and punched his chest to clear his airways. "It's a six-week trip, miss. I should think we'll not see London for another four and a bit weeks yet."

Arabella nodded having figured the same. "Will the captain not stop for supplies along the way?" If they docked, she could try to escape. It was worth the risk. The captain joked with one of the deckhands and drew her attention to his lovely mouth. A mouth that had kissed her beyond thought only hours earlier, leaving her with emotions so conflicting she'd not known what to say or how to react ever since.

Without thought she licked her lips just as he caught her eye. His mouth lifted into a knowing grin and her palms started to sweat. She shouldn't be attracted to him and had in fact protested to the very infuriating man that she never would be. But she was. Never had she found a man more attractive in her life. The reflection infuriated her as much as it excited her.

She was on a ship, in the middle of the Mediterranean, could she throw caution aside and do what she wanted for the first time in her life? Such actions went against everything she'd been brought up to believe, to think and act, but what was life without a little adventure or so others had said.

Of course, it would mean she would have to tell the

captain she wanted adventure, to live free until the time came that she was returned to her father, especially if she wanted him to kiss her again. Or maybe she'd just let him try and seduce her and let him think it was entirely his idea. Such a ploy would certainly save her pride, and yet, could she wait so long for him to kiss her again?

What a fool she was. Had she not just argued with him that she would never allow him to kiss her again? And here she was, with a little wine in her belly, moonlit night and a handsome captain at the end of a dinner table and she'd succumbed to the romance of it all.

Arabella let her gaze travel over his form and noted his hand was fisted on the table. She caught his heated, intense gaze and held it. What she was contemplating was wrong, scandalous in fact and ruining. Should she be caught, her good social standing would be a thing of the past. Her betrothed would turn away from her in disgrace.

Not that the former would bother her much. Lord Montague hadn't taken much interest in her even after the notices were posted about their forthcoming nuptials. Too interested in his friends and the enjoyment of the island life that he could experience. But Captain Blackmore was interested. And by the hooded, lazy gaze as he took his fill of her, his seduction of her would be whenever she allowed it.

The sound of her dinner companion's voice jolted her back. "The captain has enough supplies to last us until we reach England. No point trying to escape, miss. You're as stuck here on this ship as much as the rest of us."

Arabella nodded. "I thought as much." She turned toward the deckhand. "Have you ever kidnapped a woman before or am I the only lucky one?"

He laughed. "We're not even really pirates. We ship

139

contraband, smuggle sometimes into England when toffs like you require goods. The cargo has always been menial fare that wouldn't hurt a fly. So when the captain discussed taking you onboard against yer will we were all very against the idea. But the funds that are due to the captain will enable him to leave for Scotland and his crew to start a fresh life wherever we want. 'Tis only fair the amount is paid."

"And you too believe that my father owes this money?" She thought back on her papa and his penchant for gambling. It wouldn't surprise her in the least that he'd smuggled goods into England to make a profit, whether it was against the English law or not. Where there was quick blunt to be made, her father normally sniffed it out like a beagle. But to not pay a debt seemed to go against the character she thought she knew so well.

"He does. I just hope for your sake he can pay it. The men here never wanted to pull you into this mess, but the captain having seen you one day wouldn't hear sense. It was as if he—"

"Miss Hester, it's time you went back to the cabin." The captain cut into the deckhand's speech and left Arabella grappling to know what he was going to say.

"I'm not ready to go below decks. I'm having a lovely conversation with Mr...?"

The deckhand grinned. "Call me Joe."

"I'm having a lovely conversation with Joe. You retire if you wish, but I'm staying here." Arabella took a sip of wine and squealed, dropping the beverage over the table when the captain picked her up, threw her over his shoulder and started to storm toward the cabin's door. She clasped his back and realized her mistake as soon as she felt the corded muscles that ran down his spine.

The warmth of his skin penetrated his shirt, and her stomach tied into knots. He was so strong, virile that it was overwhelming. She didn't say anything else. Instead, she waited for him to place her back onto her feet so she could look at him in the eye when she gave him a proper set down.

"How dare you treat me like a piece of meat? It has been many years since I've been made to go to bed like an errant child. I may not be a Duke's daughter, but I am a well-bred, respectable woman. Does that mean anything to you?'

"I know exactly who you are." His words were low with a savage edge and the pent up desire she read in his gaze sent her heart to pound. *He was going to kiss her…*

Arabella gasped as he took her lips, using her shock to deepen the embrace. This was madness. An addictive disease that no matter how destructive, one she didn't wish to be cured of.

He nipped her lips, suckled the bottom one before pulling away. Her body wanted to melt into a puddle at his feet. Instead, she grasped his shirt and wouldn't allow the distance to go any further. "And who is that?"

He clasped the collar of her shirt and slipped it off her shoulder, revealing a good portion of skin. "The woman I want in my bed, tonight and for as many nights to come for as long as she'll allow it."

"You know what you're asking of me." Arabella cleared her throat, even to her, her voice sounded husky and nothing like the forthright, determined voice she usually sported.

His eyes darkened in determination. "I do. And yet I'm still going to ask."

He swung her into his arms and carried her over to the

bed. Could she actually do this? Throw her virginity away and possibly her future? He nuzzled her neck, his breath sending delicious shivers down her skin.

Oh yes, she could throw it all away if only he kept making her feel like this.

Special, needy and expectant, like she was the only woman in the world.

The captain clasped the hem of her shirt and ripped it off. Arabella sank into the bedding and watched enthralled as he came down over her before she realized something imperative. "Somehow this seems wrong when I don't know your first name."

He clutched her waist and idly ran a finger over her stomach. "My name's Stephen."

Stephen... It suited him. He unclasped the buttons on her buckskin breeches before touching her where no one had ever touched before. Arabella closed her eyes and reveled in the delicious friction he created against her flesh. Fire burned through her blood, a delicious ache settled between her legs and she moaned as fingers delved within her. Unable to stem her need, she lifted against his hand, wanting more of his touch.

His rumbling chuckle against her lips tickled. "You like that, do you not?" His touch shifted to her most intimate of places she gasped.

"Very much so. Tell me what you're doing to me."

"I'm kissing you. Letting you feel with my tongue, with my lips." He took her mouth in a searing kiss, dragging her further into a world she'd often wondered about, but was forever elusive. "How much I want to take you and make you mine."

Arabella slid her hand under his shirt and pulled it out of his breeches, dragging it over his head. The muscles of his shoulders flexed, his pectoral and abdomen rippled with the movement. Her mouth dried.

Magnificent.

Taking a chance, she kissed her way down his chest, before teasing a nipple with her tongue. She heard his intake of breath and stopped. "Have I hurt you?"

He pulled away, kneeling between her thighs. "Not in the way you think."

Arabella laughed as he ripped her breeches down her legs and threw them absently to the floor. His intense gaze branded her as his as he settled back over her. His hard member pushed against her mons, rubbed along her slickened heat. The friction from the soft yet rigid appendage did odd things to her insides. Her stomach twisted in delicious knots. "Yes. Keep doing that."

The tip of his member entered her and she slipped her legs up around his waist.

"You make me so desperate I can scarcely breathe."

Arabella bit her lip, loving that she could make him lose a little control. His breath was ragged and she undulated beneath him, wanting more, needing Stephen to make her his. "Is this what I'm supposed to do?" He pushed a little further in and a slight sting dampened her desire.

He nodded, rolling his hips a little as he pushed some more. "It's very good. Too good," he said, before thrusting once and taking her fully.

Arabella froze as the width and length of him wasn't what she'd expected. Deep inside, she felt full, sore, but also impatient to see what else he could do for her. She wanted to experience it all, and now wasn't soon enough.

"I'm sorry." He kissed her, swooped her into a void of need before slowly, with each thrust of tongue, matched the stroke with his hips. "I didn't want to hurt you."

The sincerity in his voice made her heart thump. "I'm well." She wrapped her arms about his neck and smiled. "Please proceed."

S tephen chuckled, but took each stroke slowly. He was large, probably too large for a virgin of her petite frame. But women like Arabella were rare and the thought of her future husband taking her in such a way, consummating their marriage wasn't to be borne.

The fop she was betrothed to wouldn't be gentle. Why, he'd more likely turn her over and sodomise her instead.

She undulated beneath him, her breasts rocking with their lovemaking, and he felt sure his choice to have her was right. Maybe not morally right, but for Arabella he'd done her a favor in showing her what it was supposed to be like for a woman when laying with a man.

Heat, the slap of skin on skin, moistness and moans were what was supposed to be heard and felt when a woman was in the throes of passion. Not silence, whimpering like he instinctively knew she would endure with Lord Montague.

"Have you ever found bliss, Arabella?"

She opened her eyes and he lost a part of himself to their crystalline beauty. "What is that? I've seen women with men before and they seem to enjoy it, but I've never done anything like this before."

"The fact that you do not know is all the answer I need." He rolled onto his back and pulled her to straddle his waist. He'd not thought she could be any more beautiful, but above, him, in control of their enjoyment, she was magnificent.

She braced herself on top of him, her hands idly feeling the hair on his chest. "Is this position even possible?"

"Absolutely. Just lift yourself as if you're riding a horse, but bring yourself down on me. Nice and slowly, but continuously. I promise you'll enjoy it." He clasped her hips and helped her, as the first few movements were awkward. It didn't take her long before she'd mastered the sexual position.

Stephen bit the inside of his lip as she rode him, her hips swaying slightly that matched her bountiful breasts. He shut his eyes not needing to see the stimulating picture she made. He wouldn't come until she'd found her own pleasure, and by the increased pants and slickness between them, it wouldn't be long.

A self-satisfied smile tweaked his lips knowing she was enjoying this as much as he.

"Yes, keep doing that." Oh God, she was going to kill him. Her body, tight and willing drew him along, pulled at his cock and made him want to blow between her legs. How did she learn so quickly? "Ride me until you come. Use me."

The sight of her fondling her own breast was too much. Stephen swore. He couldn't take much more. She rode him, her strokes consistent and mind numbing.

Stephen grabbed her hips, helped her to come down hard with each stroke. Her gaze went hazy with awe. "Is that good?" he panted, knowing it felt bloody fantastic.

"Yes," she gasped. "Oh yes it is."

Their speed increased. The sound of skin slapping skin echoed throughout the space along with the scent of sex and still he urged her on, wanting to see her shatter for the very first time in his arms. It didn't take long.

Arabella moaned, her head flopping back as she rode him through her release. Stephen, leaving one hand on her hips, clasped her breast and tweaked a pinkened, erect nipple. She gasped again, her body convulsing around his cock and dragging him along to join her.

Lights blazed behind his eyes as his body released days of pent up desire. He took her without heed or care, allowed them both to come apart within each other's arms.

Arabella collapsed beside him, both their breathing ragged. Not willing to let her scoot away, he pulled her into the nook of his shoulder to keep her close.

"I'm…speechless," she said, sighing and sounding sleepy.

Stephen laughed. She was more than speechless. She was thoroughly ruined and by him. Never had he felt more like a cad or like someone who'd given a precious gift to a woman who otherwise may have never known the pleasure that could be had between two people. "And now you know."

She looked up at him and the trust he read in her gaze unsettled him a little. "What?"

"What pleasure is." He grinned at the blush that stole over her cheeks. How after what they'd just done she could be embarrassed he had no clue. "I gather you rather enjoyed it."

Arabella grinned and started to play with his chest hair. "I did. Rather a lot, I'm afraid. Which could be a bad thing."

"How so?" He didn't think such a thing could ever be bad, especially if he had her before him, opening for him, beckoning him with her gaze. His cock twitched at the thought.

"Because I'll want to do it again." She held his gaze, not an ounce of fear in her declaration.

Relief poured through him that he'd not scared her off. "Well, I'm never one to disappoint a lady."

She raised her brow and threw him a knowing grin. "Not with sex it would seem."

"Touché. Not with sex at least." He laughed, rolling her onto his back and taking her again. With each kiss, each embrace or touch they shared, Stephen felt his life changing, growing brighter, clearer than ever before. Arabella was delightful, a willing companion in his bed, laughed and took charge when she wanted. She was a breath of fresh air in a life that had stagnated a long time ago.

CHAPTER 6

The next few weeks passed in a haze of desire, stolen moments and laughter.

Arabella couldn't remember when she'd had a more delightful time in her life. Somehow, Stephen brought out the best in her in what could possibly be the worst time of her life. Which was interesting since he was the root of her problems or at least, part of them.

Stephen changed his mind as to their destination and had sailed past the entrance to the Thames river and had instead, continued along the English coast toward Cornwall. Today they were anchoring off a remote cove where a small village could be seen scattered back from the land behind. A magnificent house further up the coast looked over the township and rocky outcrop that made up part of the coast. She stood beside the wheel and watched the men go about their jobs. They were so close to home. It had been months since she'd set foot on English soil.

Arabella frowned, not knowing how seeing England again made her feel. She supposed a little sad that her voyage with Stephen was ending. That soon he would hand her over to her father once the debt was paid, and her betrothed if he would still have her, which she hoped he would not. The thought of laying with another man other than Stephen made her stomach roil in dread.

Lord Montague and their impending marriage floated through her mind. Did he know of her disappearance? Had her father somehow managed word to him and even now, were both in pursuit to rescue her? She scoffed, doubting his lordship cared a fig what happened to her person. His only concern would be for the money he'd lose in not marrying her.

She bit her lip to stop her eyes from welling up. The thought of being removed from Stephen's side and embarking on a life she had promised another left her hollow. She didn't even know Lord Montague. Had hardly spent any time being acquainted when he was in Malta with her family. The image of laying under him, making love as a wife should with her husband brought revulsion coursing through her blood. If she were lucky, his lordship would not want someone who is sullied, would look elsewhere for a wife. Such hope didn't last long, not when her marriage portion was large enough to forgive any misdemeanor by her.

Footsteps sounded behind her and she knew by the fall of the boot who it was without turning. Strong arms encircled her waist and she settled against his chest the fresh smell of the ocean and soap coming with him. "Do you wish to join me on the mainland? It may be nice for you to be on land for a little while."

"I would love to." She turned and pushed the lock of hair out of his face. A few of the crew smiled in their direction, some making light of the captain's public show of affection. Arabella reveled in it, loving how he had no qualms in kissing or touching her anywhere on the ship and before anyone. "How long do you think your business will take?"

"A day or so. No more." He walked her backward and the cool wood of the railing sat against her back. "Why? Impatient to get me back in our cabin?"

She slapped his chest but undulated against his hardness, loving the fact he now called his quarters *their* quarters. "Of course not. Whatever gave you that impression?" He laughed and shook his head. Over the last few weeks, a closeness had formed between them. One that she'd not thought possible, especially with how they were thrown together in the first place. With Stephen by her side, Arabella felt free, more herself than any other time she can remember. There were no rules with him, no must and must not's in life.

"You have a certain look in your eye, one where I believe you'd like nothing more than to take me somewhere private and do wickedly naughty things to me," he grinned, a devilish light in his eyes.

"No I do not. You're simply imagining things. Now come, we're getting closer to the coast and I need to change into appropriate clothing for a woman." Not that she'd like to change out of her breeches, loose fitting shirt and jacket. Never had she ever been so comfortable in clothing in her life. The fact she could get about with ease and with little fuss was liberating.

"Of course. Lead the way, my dear. Any excuse helping you change."

Arabella laughed. "You're incorrigible." But she pulled him along with her in any case.

· · ·

They anchored late in the afternoon, just as the sun started to disappear behind darkened clouds to the west. It was only a short boat journey to the quaint town. Thatched roofed homes and walls that were made of wood and plaster ran along the foreshore a little back from the beach. Children scooted about playing, some people walked along the cobbled streets entering a few stores that sold particular goods. A highly polished carriage was being unhitched and unloaded at the Boar and Hound Inn. It was a lovely location, very English and welcoming.

Arabella followed Stephen up a side street off the main thoroughfare and was surprised to see an old woman standing on the street beside a cottage door smiling at them. He jogged toward her and picked up the lady and spun her about, laughing. Arabella stopped and just watched. From the love and jovial exclamations the woman was making, she gathered his important business was seeing his mother or some relative.

Stephen gestured for her to join them, and her heart squeezed that he would include her in this. The older woman was a lovely lady, very welcoming and happy to see her son. Introductions were performed and they took afternoon tea with his mother. Arabella considered the lady's perfect manners and impeccable speech which seemed at odds to her sons employment. Again she wondered who Stephen really was and what his history had been. Something told her he wasn't only just a pirate.

They weren't able to stay long much to her surprise. Stephen had other business at the inn, but he promised his mother he would visit again and discuss all that was necessary then. Arabella bid farewell, but was unsure as to what

Stephen had meant. What was necessary with his life and what did it have to do with his mother?

A short time later, they walked into the taproom of the inn. Arabella looked about while Stephen organized a private dining chamber. The room was dim, with a burning fire that sat directly across from the bar. Stephen threw orders about like a seasoned gentleman of the *ton*, and once more Arabella was struck by how commanding, autocratic he was. Their weeks together had brought them close in every sense except in the one way that mattered most to her. Who was this man? What had happened in his past that he now sailed the high seas for a living?

He was still a mystery. She knew nothing of his past, of his life outside the captioning the ship or what he'd like to do in the future. And today with his mother only confirmed her suspicions he was hiding something.

But what? And why?

The innkeeper, an elderly, rotund man led them off into a little room that had a roaring fire and a beautiful view of the seaside beyond.

Small vessels dotted the shallow coastal water and Arabella stepped over toward the fire to warm herself. Stephen sank with a sigh into a settee and shut his eyes. The storm that had been on the horizon earlier in the day was starting to show its presence as the wind picked up and rain started to spatter against the windowpane.

"You said you have other business here. Are you meeting someone else?"

Stephen ran a hand through his hair making it stand on end. He cocked one eye open. "I am. Yes. He should be here after dinner, which should be served soon." He gestured to the seat beside him. "Come. Sit with me."

Arabella sat, not liking how he seemed a little ill at ease. "Is something troubling you?"

He pulled out a missive and passed it to her. It was from Lord Montague. She started for a moment before tearing the missive open.

C *aptain,*

I'm shocked that you would steal away the woman who is to become my wife in only a few weeks' time. I should imagine if you're reading this missive you should also be looking over your shoulder as I'm going to have my revenge on you.

If one hair is misplaced on Miss Hester's head I shall have great enjoyment hurting you in any torturous way possible. It is well advised that the moment you make land in England you hand over my betrothed immediately if I'm not there to make you do so. Not that by doing so will alter the course of your future. You will hang for this crime, you dirty pirate scum.

That is one promise I will make and hold true.

Lord Montague.

A rabella screwed up the letter and threw it into the fire. Fear spiked through her at being ripped away from the one man she'd ever cared for. To be placed with peer who held her in little regard other than monetary value.

Stephen didn't say anything, just watched her as she fiddled with her skirts. "I suppose we should discuss what you're planning to do with me and when you're going to be rid of me as well."

"And if I don't want to be rid of you. What then?" He

turned and met her gaze fully, his eyes as bleak as her own emotions. "Will you leave me anyway, Arabella?"

She stood, needing space. "You know I cannot stay. They will kill you if they ever caught you. The banns have been called, here and in Malta. Everyone knows I'm to marry Lord Montague. You seek revenge on my father, you're using me for leverage to gain payment. That fact is not something to be passed over and ignored."

"I know that." He stood, towering over her and her body yearned to lean into him, wrap her arms about his neck and kiss them both senseless. To kiss their problems into oblivion. "Perhaps knowing what your father owes me for will make things clearer for you."

"Please. Enlighten me." She crossed her arms over her chest needing any defense she could gather just in case what Stephen told her was devastating. Just one look at Stephen pulled her into a world that wasn't where she belonged. He was impossible to ignore.

"I'm a smuggler by trade, have been since the man you're about to meet after dinner gifted me his ship. Your father sought me out and asked me to smuggle into England a large shipment of silk to be sold in the markets of London. I should imagine most of the upper ten-thousand are wearing what your father shipped illegally into this country using my men and my ship. The payment due was to be the last monetary amount needed to give them and their families a comfortable life. Better than anything they've ever dreamed of. Your father has stolen this from them and I'm not going to allow that to happen."

Arabella sat back down. "I don't understand. Father has money so why he's refused to pay what was due, illegal or otherwise doesn't make sense. How much is the debt?"

A muscle worked in Stephen's jaw and trepidation settled like a rock in her gut. "Two thousand pounds."

"But he has that." Doesn't he? Of late they had been having food that was less extravagant than usual. Come to think of it, less servants and only one carriage to support their household in Malta. Was her father short of blunt? Were they poor? She swallowed.

"Apparently not," he said.

"What will you do if he cannot pay?" Would he ruin her publicly? Throw her overboard as a waste of his effort and time? She shook the silly thought aside, her mind going places that were less than helpful. At times such as these one needed a clear mind, free to think rationally.

"I will ruin him." *And you as well.* The unspoken words hung between them like a noose.

She clasped his hand. "Perhaps if I speak to my father I can get him to pay you and there be no need for any further trouble." Although the more Arabella thought about the strictures of her life of late, something told her that her father wasn't going to be able to pay no matter how much she wished it.

A knock sounded at the door before a tall man, dressed in attire Arabella had only ever seen in the highest ranks of society. In her shabby dress, stained and torn in parts it left her feeling inadequate and poor. She checked her gown, pleating a section of her skirt to try and hide the small tear.

The gentleman's eyes widened when he spotted her, but he continued into the room and greeted Stephen with warmth. Who was he?

"And who is this?" the man asked, nodding toward her.

Arabella frowned, not liking how this gentleman's tone lacked warmth when speaking of her.

"This is Miss Arabella Hester. Sir Ronald Hester's

daughter." Stephen turned to her. "Arabella, this is Gabriel Lyons, the Duke of Dale."

She felt her mouth fall open and she nodded in hello. How was it Stephen knew a duke?

"*Miss* Arabella, is it?" The word was accentuated and had it been as sharp like a knife, she didn't hesitate to think Stephen would've been cut. "As in unmarried and from looking about this room and seeing no maid I can assume, unchaperoned..." The duke sighed. "I had hoped the rumors were false."

For the first time since she'd known Stephen he looked sheepish. "Dinner is about to be served. We'll discuss this later. Alone."

The gentlemen glared at each other and Arabella sat down at the wooden table as dinner was brought in by two kitchen girls. Night was falling and the storm howled outside. Candles were brought in and the fire stoked to ward off the dark chill of the night. The windows whistled, a cold draft running down her spine and making her flimsy gown less than ideal in such weather. She shivered, wishing she had a shawl or blanket.

"We'll be staying here for the night," Stephen said, as if sensing her unvoiced concern. He joined her at the table, but didn't meet her eye. The other gentleman did the same and a quiet awkwardness settled around them. The duke did not try and hide his disappointment at seeing her here. She quickly ate the stew and welcomed the maid who came in to take her upstairs. Bidding the men goodnight, she left them to their discussions.

"What the hell is going on? Rumors reached me in London over your escapades or should I say your kidnapping of innocent women. What are you doing?" Anger thrummed in the duke's voice and Stephen tempered his answer.

He slumped back in his chair and sighed. "Her father owes me funds. She's my leverage in getting it." He didn't point out that the day he'd gone to Arabella's father to ask for the blunt in a gentlemanlike manner, he'd spotted her in the garden and his whole plan to be civil had dissolved before his eyes. She'd been sitting on a bench, surrounded by lush green plants and he'd wanted her instantly. Had abruptly turned about and devised a more devious plan that would enable him to have her in his bed and alone for some weeks.

He was a cad.

And revenge was sweet. What he hadn't planned on was how the lovable woman with a strong backbone and warmth could worm her way under his ribs. He rubbed his chest, his like for her much more than he'd ever thought possible.

"She's a gentleman's daughter. You'll ruin her, if you haven't already. You are better than this, Stephen. I know you have peerage in your family. You need to act the gentleman, now man, before it's too late." The duke rubbed his jaw, his face all hard angles and serious.

The disappointment in his friend's tone ripped him in two. Was he better than this? His family had lost every-thing before he was even born. He'd never been given the opportunity to know what it was like to be lord and master of all he surveyed. To care for people as only a member of the upper ten-thousand should. So was he really better than a smuggling pirate who idled his life away on the sea? "You've always held me in too higher regard, Gabe. And let's not forget the woman you married was an innocent on her way back to England when you seduced her, in front of us all. How is what I'm doing any different?"

"I married Eloise, that's how it's different." The duke's face softened, but for only a moment. "It also doesn't hurt that I'm the Duke of Dale. You must take Miss Hester back to London and find another way to gain payment from her father."

Stephen cringed at the thought. He didn't want to return her. And what the hell did that mean if he did not? Did he feel more for Arabella than he was admitting to himself? They certainly worked well together in bed, but in everyday life was another matter entirely. All Stephen knew was he was not ready for her to leave him. Not yet at least. "I will not. She stays with me until payment is made in full. I have nothing left to lose. But I'll be damned if I'll let my men suffer the same fate."

"You can still lose your life. Think man, not even I could save you from the noose should you be caught. And I haven't told you everything I've heard. There is more you need to know."

Stephen sat forward, frowning. "What don't I know?"

"Lord Montague has sailed after you and is headed here. Been tipped off somehow as to your location I would think. From what I could find out, he's crossed paths with Sir Hester who is now accompanying him. By tomorrow afternoon your captive's betrothed will be here to collect his bride-to-be." He paused, shaking his head. "This is absurd behavior. You know better than this." The duke gestured with his hands and looked ready to throttle him at his continued silence. "What possessed you?"

Stephen crossed his arms over his chest. "I will not be threatened by a fellow who likes to be buggered every night in the hells of London. A lifetime with me would be sweeter than a day with him. Why, he'd never even see her. Not the real, Arabella. He would only ever view her as a woman who took his freedom away. A woman who'll never be a man; the sex he desires most." He could not give Arabella over to such a fate. To sail away knowing he would never see her again and that he'd left her to life a life she would never enjoy.

A muscle worked at the duke's temple. "Whether the rumors are true or not, she's promised to him. Should he come here, you'd be best to hand her over and make your way to Scotland where the law will not find you too quickly or better yet, will forget your indiscretion. You know what Lord Montague is like. He's a prick with a lot of connections. Forget the blunt you're owed. Your life is worth more than a couple thousand pounds."

Stephen swallowed. Gabe was right in many respects. He should never have kidnapped Arabella in the first place. He pinched his nose. What the hell had gotten into him? But it still didn't change the fact he couldn't regret the decision he made. He would never regret his time with Arabella. They were the best times of his pitiful life so far. "I won't let her go."

"Even if Lord Montague is willing to settle the debt? What will your excuse be then to keep her?"

"It won't come to that. I shouldn't think Lord Montague wants to marry her that badly, especially as she's not his preferred type." Stephen took a long swig of his brandy. "If the debt is paid, of course I'll have to let her go. What reason would I have to keep her here then?" *Other than love…*

The duke nodded, his gaze compassionate. "Indeed."

"Tomorrow we should know." Stephen pushed away the thought that tonight could possibly be the last time he was ever with Arabella. Such musings didn't warrant thinking over.

"That you're having dinner with the chit, conversing with her and no doubt warming her bed at night tells me your indifference to what tomorrow could bring is false." He sighed. "That is all I'll say on the matter, but you need to take care. This could end badly for her and yourself." The duke leaned back in his chair. "As you know, Eloise is with child and I must leave you tomorrow morn, but should you need me, you know where I am."

Stephen nodded. "Aye. I know and I thank you." He poured them both another brandy and settled back in his chair changing the subject to discuss their mutual interests in investments in London. He tried to concentrate on what his friend was saying, but his mind kept venturing upstairs to where Arabella slept waiting for him...

...possibly for the very last time.

He inwardly swore and left the duke, mouth agape, alone to converse with himself.

She was asleep when he made it up to their room. The moonlight cast a hazy shade of blue over the covers highlighting her silky, white skin. Her hair looked ebony and cascaded over the pillows to frame her beautiful face. The bedding had slipped low on her chest, giving him an ample view of her nakedness and his cock twitched.

He sighed knowing he'd made a mess of things. He should never have kidnapped her and dragged her back to England with the sole purpose of ruining her and her family. Because now, that's exactly what would happen should the scandal break out across London.

If it hadn't already.

She fidgeted in sleep and her eyes fluttered open. She sat up and kneeled on the bed, beckoning him to join her. Stephen needed no cajoling and went to her willingly, took her mouth in a searing kiss and dragged them both into an inferno of desire.

After the weeks of being together, she'd learned a few things and quickly she disposed of his jacket, pulling his shirt out of his trews before sliding her hand inside and clasping his ass.

Stephen grinned through her fun. His body ached to take her, to lift her up and impale her on his hardened shaft. Playfully she pushed him away a little and slowly lifted her shift, exposing a body that had captivated him from the first moment he'd seen it.

Unable to stop himself he toppled her onto the bed and wrapped her legs about his waist. His cock slid against her moistened heat, teasing them both for what was to come.

Them. Literally.

She sighed his name and his control snapped. He thrust within her over and over again, the frenzied need thrumming through him unable to sate. She met his every stroke with awe, her gasps, moans for more and scoring nails down his back only making the interlude hotter, more enjoyable.

Her fingers tangled in his hair, tugging slightly. Stephen kissed his way down her neck, slender shoulder to eventually pay homage to her breasts. A lovely handful with nipples the color of roses on a summer's day.

She squirmed as his kisses moved farther down her

person. Her stomach was smooth, soft and a beacon for more delights. Stephen pushed her legs apart, inhaling her sweet scent before kissing the glistening flesh before him.

"What are you doing? You can't do that."

He chuckled at the shocked but inquisitive tenor of her voice. "Lay back. Relax and let me love you."

Gradually the muscles in her legs relaxed. To have her, laying before him, open and trusting was the most delicious elixir he'd ever tasted. He licked her swollen bud and she gasped, her fingers clasping his head for purchase.

He loved her with his tongue, welcomed the rhythm she found undulating against his face. He added his hand to her lovemaking and took her with his fingers. Arabella lost all inhibitions and Stephen's body ached with the need to have her. How he adored her reaction to him, her enjoyment as great as his own. He groaned as her body tightened and then convulsed under his touch.

"That's it," he said, sucking on her hardened nub. "Come for me. Enjoy me as much as I am enjoying you." She whimpered under him, their lovemaking climaxing to a frenzy unlike any he'd ever experienced before. Arabella called his name and she came apart in his arms.

Stephen's body roared with the need to have her now. He sat up and flipped her over onto her stomach, before coming down over her back licking his way up her spine as he thrust deep into her hot wet core. The delighted gasp sent shivers to wrack his body. Sweat poured over his skin.

His release flowed through every limb, every pore before lights burst before his eyes as he came inside her. They laid like that for a while both lost in the exquisite torture that they had just endured. He slumped down next to her and pulled her against his chest, wanting her as close as he possibly could get to the woman in his arms.

She wrapped her arms around his body. "That was amazing Stephen. I can't imagine ever finding that with anybody else. Please tell me you do not experience this each time you lay with other women?"

Stephen shut his eyes. Did he experience this with other women when he slept with them? Something told him deep down inside is soul he didn't. That he'd never experienced anything so mind numbingly good in his eight and twenty years. "No. Never like this."

He felt rather than saw her smile against his chest. "Good."

CHAPTER 7

Arabella woke to the delicious sight of Stephen's bottom going into his breeches as he pulled them on. She lay there silently, loving the peaceful quietness of the morning and just the two of them being alone like a married couple partaking in a holiday by the seaside.

She shouldn't delude herself. All of it, their time together, the enjoyment they brought to one another, wasn't real. It wouldn't last. How could it when she was to marry another and Stephen had plans of his own future?

He busied himself about the room, pulling on his shirt, his boots, tying a cravat. There was no doubt she didn't know everything about him, but given time she was sure she would find out. Not that any time was left. Tears threatened and she blinked quickly, not wanting him to see her upset.

Not entirely certain of what he would do with her, she pushed the worrisome thoughts aside and continued to take pleasure in the view. Stephen bent over and his pants pulled tight. A smiled lifted her lips. He really was the most handsome rogue she'd ever seen.

And he was hers to enjoy, if only for the day.

He turned and caught her staring. A knowing eyebrow rose as he strode toward the bed. "Like what you see, Miss Hester?"

She kneeled and let the sheet fall to the bed. He stilled, his muscles tightening as if preparing to launch and tackle her to the ground. The thought of what he did to her, the pleasure each touch wrought made the imagining longed for. "As a matter of fact I do." She pulled him closer by the waist of his pants. "In fact, perhaps you would be inclined to forgo whatever business takes you from me and join me here for some other mutual satisfaction."

He chuckled, his touch idly gliding up and down her back. She shivered and let her own hand venture over his frontfalls. He cock hardened against her palm and her body warmed in response.

"I want you, Stephen." A muscle twitched in his jaw before, without any notice, he flipped her onto her back, came down on top of her and ground himself against her. Arabella gasped at the contact, wanting, needing him close. The non-existent distance too much to bear.

He ripped at his frontfalls, lifted her a little and thrust into her aching core and carried them both toward bliss within moments. She came up to meet him, to join with him as deep as possible. He filled her completely, made her whole and she moaned when he slowed his pace to tease relentlessly.

"Don't stop," she gasped. He didn't, just inexorably kept up his torturous pace.

"I won't," he whispered against her ear. "Not until you ask me to." He nipped her lobe, his hands either side of her skull. She met his gaze and almost drowned in his sensual haze. They watched each other as both fell into bliss. The delicious spasms that rocked through her body left her sated and sleepy. Arabella kissed his shoulder, loving the feel of Stephen above her, in her, with her.

"I never knew it could be like this for a woman. That being with a man could be so enjoyable."

Stephen's lips curved and then he laughed. "If the man's doing it right of course it can. I'm glad I'm able to pleasure you." He laid beside her, pulling her into the crook of his arm. "You're a very intelligent, beautiful woman who deserves only the best of all things."

Arabella looked up and held his gaze. "I'm glad you think so. Thank you."

He nodded. "I do. Don't ever think otherwise."

She snuggled into his hold, not wanting him to see that she'd become a watering pot since last night. The realization that she did not want to leave Stephen hit her like gale force wind on the stormy seas. He was everything she wanted in life. A man who listened to her, loved her with reverence and only wanted what was best. And soon she would have to leave him. Family duty told her so, along with marriage contracts, but the thought of never seeing him again tore her in two.

Broke her heart in fact.

CHAPTER 8

Stephen crossed his arms over his chest and glared at the pompous Lord Montague, who stood on the deck of his own ship, similarly glaring. "So what do we owe the pleasure, my lord? I didn't think the coastal communities of Cornwall would pull such a gentleman of the *ton* to its ports. You'll find no Almacks here."

His lordship snarled and Stephen laughed. He almost didn't recognize Lord Montague. In the months since he'd seen him, he'd grown larger, more pompous and red-faced. "Where is Miss Hester? I'm here to take her home. We're to be married next week." His voice was high, too high for a man.

"Take a breath lad. You are allowed to breathe you know." Stephen leaned against the railing and heard the footsteps of two of his crewmen come to stand behind him. Lord Montague for all his feminine characteristics had two very beefy crew members watching the proceedings from behind his lordship. It didn't tax Stephen's imagination to know the men were trouble. It was best to have his own protection in situations like these.

An older man he recognized as Arabella's father appeared on deck and waddled over to where her betrothed stood. "Where is my daughter? I demand you release her at once."

Lord Montague lifted his overly long nose in the air. "Do not assume I'm here to spar with you. I'm here for my betrothed and nothing more. Now, where is she?"

"Safe." Stephen raised his brow. "Next question."

"It's not a question but a command. Bring her to me post haste and no further action will be taken against you. Not by me at least."

Arabella's father huffed out a breath. "I, on the other hand, will ensure you pay for this treachery."

"I look forward to it, Sir Hester," Stephen said. "But pray tell me, Lord Montague, why is it that a man of your ilk wishes to marry at all? I always thought your tastes veered in another direction entirely."

His lordships face turned crimson. "You have one hour to produce Miss Hester or I'll not be held responsible for what happens to you, your men or your ship."

Stephen waved the man's threats away. "An hour? But I have to say my goodbyes and we're forgetting one very important factor in all this. The payment that is due to me." Lord Montague nodded to one of his men who quickly ran off. The fact that the payment of two thousand pounds was only moments away should accelerate the blood pumping through Stephens veins. He should be happy, elated that his men would have the future they'd worked so hard to grasp.

It didn't. If anything the thought of the payment was like the bemoaning sound of a church death knell. It meant the end of his time with Arabella. Panic mixed with pain coursed through his gut. He may never see her again.

Kiss lips that bespoke of sin and felt like silk. Listen to the intelligent quick wit that had captured his attention from the very first.

He would miss her, and something deep within his mind whispered that he'd do a lot more than that. He'd be only half of himself without her.

I love her.

The realization struck him like a sword to the throat. He loved her? The words that should frighten him didn't. Instead they fit him like a new pair of leather boots.

The brute who ran off returned.

"Give Captain Blackmore the bag," Lord Montague said without emotion.

Arabella's father gestured at the bag as it was handed over. "I had the funds in Malta, should you have just asked, none of this would've been necessary against my daughter. But like the thieving, kidnapping scoundrel that you are, you couldn't wait like any other patient man. No. Instead you kidnapped an innocent woman and tried to ruin her reputation."

Stephen's eyes narrowed as his temper started to spike. "I don't take well to liars, and you Sir Hester, are one of those. I have waited a good twelve months for this payment, none of which was forthcoming until today and not until I had to take action totally against my better judgment or character." He fought the ill ease that sat in his gut. Yes, he'd waited months for payment, but the action to kidnap Arabella couldn't be laid at anyone's door but his own. And sinner that he was, he'd enjoyed every damn moment with the lass.

Stephen's second in command took the bag and rifled through it. "Looks to be all here, Captain."

Stephen nodded. "Put it below decks."

Lord Montague stepped forward. "Your time is running out Captain Blackmore. I want to see my betrothed. Now." Stephen raised his brow at the man's attempt to sound threatening. What a sad little specimen his lordship was.

"Go fetch Arabella and gather up anything she has at the inn and on the ship. She's leaving forthwith," Stephen barked out the order to a member of his crew and hated the way his voice strained over the word 'leaving'.

His lordship smirked. "I'm so glad you've seen reason. Common sense is not something I would associate with a pirate, but in your case and in this instance you seem to have some."

"I would shut up and rightly so, Lord Montague, before I'm tempted to step onto your ship and cut off the one appendage you love most. And as for you, Sir Hester. I'm not without connections also, with a few whispered words I could ruin you in London. Best you shut up as well."

Both men paled and didn't reply.

It took an hour or so for Arabella to be rowed out to the anchored ships. During the time the men on both ships stood about, patiently waiting, but always on alert. Stephen watched as she climbed up the rope latter and came to stand beside him on his deck. She had a small bag clasped in her hand and a becoming flush on her cheeks. Her hair curled about her shoulders, accentuating the lovely curve of her neck. His body tightened at the sight of her. Possibly his last.

His mind fought a war within itself. Could he ask her to leave all that she aspired to, had promised herself, to marry him instead? To live in Scotland, an isolated wilderness far from the polished delights of London for the rest of her days?

And what about the funds? Was it more important to him and his men than Arabella?

He inwardly swore at the crossroad he now found himself and having no idea on which direction to take.

The sound of excited voices from the street below woke Arabella with a start. She scrambled out of bed and ran to the window to see what was happening. From the room's view, she could see Stephen's ship anchored off the bay, with another ship close beside it.

Trepidation clawed at her innards over who was docked beside him although she could probably guess. The distance not so very far, she could make out Stephen on his deck surrounded by his crewmen. The gentleman on the other ship remained unknown.

Arabella dressed and went to leave, only to find her room door locked. Concern for Stephen warred with annoyance at his high-handedness at locking her in again.

Going back to the window she watched as the two men traded words to one another. She narrowed her eyes trying to focus better, and swore when the other gentleman turned and she recognized Lord Montague.

Blast and the devil he was here and if the tubby gentleman coming to stand beside him was any indication, so was her father!

The thought of his lordship organizing a rescue almost made her laugh. Lord Montague was a man who loathed anything remotely distasteful. No doubt a rescue where his coattails could become sullied was classed as such.

Their appearance could only mean one thing. She was leaving. And did she even wish to any longer? Being with Stephen had been an exciting journey she'd never thought possible. It may not have started out too well, but the nights of pleasure and days of adventure had soon brought them together and for her at least, made her see him in a different perspective.

He was everything to her. Meant the world to her.

I love him…

One of Stephen's men broke away and started down the rope ladder, getting into the small wooden craft tied to the ship before rowing toward shore. Arabella fumbled about for her meagre belongings just in case Stephen wished her to come aboard.

She stopped what she was doing and realized where her thoughts had taken her. She loved him, that she was certain, but to leave with him? Embark on a life that was as uncertain as the weather was another thing entirely.

Could she do it? Really? Could she choose love and adventure, losing all that she'd been brought up to be, a respectable, steady lady with morals for Stephen?

A knock sounded at her door just as she slipped on a pair of boots.

"The captain wishes you to join him on the ship, Miss Hester," a firm male voice said from behind the wood.

He unlocked the door and Arabella followed the deck-hand. The trip out to the ship was reasonably quick and the closer they came, the easier it was to hear the two men and their war of words. Curses that were new to her, even after all the months on board a pirate's ship, volleyed from one boat to another. She shook her head at the absurdness.

Really. Men could be so immature at times.

"Gentleman, stop. Enough of this madness." Arabella

climbed up the rope ladder and turned to Lord Montague as she made the deck. She smiled in welcome to her father. "What are you doing here? It never occurred to me that you would chase us down."

"You speak, daughter, as if you've enjoyed the company of the blasted rogue." Her father threw a disgusted look at Stephen. "Come aboard and quickly. The sooner we have you away from this man the better."

She didn't move as an abundance of thoughts, feelings and questions bombarded her mind. Not the least of them being how unwelcome Lord Montague's presence was now that he'd actually appeared. He was a sickly color, as if the rocking motion of the boat didn't mesh well with his stomach.

"Miss Hester, we're to return to London forthwith where with any luck, notice of your prolonged stay with Captain Blackmore will be washed away like the tide. We're to marry next week."

Stephen scoffed. "I can't help but think Arabella's fall from grace would suit you well. Admit it man, you don't want to marry her. And you know damn well as to why."

Arabella started at his words. She frowned. "Why wouldn't his lordship wish to marry me? I'm not abhorrent."

He looked from her to Lord Montague, his face more thunderous than the day she'd thrown the mop overboard. "Please enlighten us, my lord."

Her betrothed pulled at his neckcloth, sweat forming on his brow. "Don't be absurd. I love Miss Hester." His lordship gestured for her to come aboard. "Join me, my dear. We'll leave directly. Now that Captain Blackmore has been paid in full there is no more reason for you to stay."

Arabella raised her brow. Stephen already had the funds? So his use of her was at an end unless…

Stephen closed the short distance between them and clasped her hands. "You don't have to go. Stay with me. Be with me." His voice was low, desperate almost.

Hope bloomed in her chest. The image of a future with him was tempting. She doubted there would be a moment of boredom. He excited her, discussed things with her as an equal. Didn't treat her as some silly nitwit girl so many men seemed to do. And he was her lover…

Her father jumped from one ship to the other and strode toward her. Arabella shut her mouth with a snap not knowing her father could be so agile when so large. "Daughter, a word in private if you will." He took her arm and pulled her a good distance away from Stephen. "What is this madness? You cannot possibly be thinking of staying with this pirate." He spat the word out like salty seawater. "Your life is with me and your future husband. I command you to leave with us at once."

She stepped back and crossed her arms. "Why must I? What I feel for the captain far outweighs what I've ever felt for Lord Montague. And you're wealthy, there is no reason for me to marry his lordship. We could make up some sort of excuse as to my disappearance from society. Say I stayed in Malta due to some sickly ailment or some such."

"Don't be absurd child. You cannot just disappear!" Her father waved his hands about in agitation. "I think it's time to tell you as to why you must leave." He sighed. "My pockets are to let. Other than the house in London, which I transferred into your name two years ago, nothing we own will remain ours unless you marry Lord Montague." Her father pulled out his handkerchief and wiped his brow, his face a deep ruddy color. "I've gambled us into a vicious debt that I cannot pay. Your betrothed has promised all vowels will be paid in full should you marry him. I owe a lot of men a lot of blunt."

So it was true. Her father was a liar and a gambler and they were poor. Despair washed over her knowing she couldn't let her father become ruined. "Why would Lord Montague do this for us? I certainly don't believe it's because he's in love with me." Her father licked his lips in agitation. "Answer me, Father?"

He sighed. "The reasons behind Lord Montague wishing to marry you are his and only his. He has not shared them with me. When the contracts were signed, let me assure you, both of us were pleased with the outcome. You will have a good life with him."

"I still don't see why I should go. So we're not as wealthy as we used to be, but there are worse prospects for people I'm sure. You can live with me and Captain Blackmore," she pleaded, wanting to hold onto her dream of marrying Stephen, if he'd have her.

Tears welled in her father's eyes and Arabella's heart twisted. "Would you see me in a poor house? After all the years I raised you, loved you only as a father can and you would turn your back on me when I needed you most. Please, Arabella, don't do this to me. Please marry his lordship. I beg of you."

Pounding started to thump across her brow. She rubbed her temples to try and alleviate the pain. She couldn't betray her father. Yes, he'd made mistakes, but he'd been the best parent anyone could ask for. She could not allow his future to be uncertain and unpleasant. She nodded, family duty outweighing that of her heart's desire. "I will do as you ask. Go back to the ship and I'll join you shortly."

He nodded, wiping his eyes before waddling off.

Stephen joined her and the worry she could read in his eyes tore at her heart. Tore at her own for that matter. "Our time has been wonderful and I thank you for it, but you know I cannot stay. I must go." Arabella tried to keep her voice strong, determined, but even she could hear the wavering tempo of devastation in it.

He stared at her in shocked silence for a moment. "Why can you not? I may not be able to give you a position, title or extreme wealth, but you have my heart. Is that not enough?"

Arabella bit her lip. Had he just told her he loved her? Tears welled in her eyes and her knees threatened to give way. He loved her. "I've already broken too many vows. One major one being with you, enjoying you in the way only a wife should enjoy a husband. I cannot break my understanding with Lord Montague as well. The banns have been called. All of London is expecting me to become his wife. My father—"

"Is no longer with funds as I said once before, but now has decided to use this against you to make you marry a man you do not love." Stephen shook her a little. "You cannot do this, Arabella. Not to yourself. You deserve better than this." Desperation tinged his tone and his eyes beseeched her to see sense.

"He's my father." Tears spilled over knowing she was leaving the man she loved. A man who loved her. She sniffed. "I cannot break my promise."

Stephen rubbed his jaw, shaking his head. "Stop and think for a moment. Why would a wealthy man marry a poor woman when he does not have to? He does not love you, so why the need to marry? Perhaps on your journey back to the capitol you should ask your father to explain this phenomenon." Sarcasm laced his tone and Arabella frowned. What was he getting at?

"What are you trying to say? That my father is in some way blackmailing Lord Montague? His lordship is above reproach. There is nothing my father could use against him." Arabella started toward the other ship. How could Stephen think so lowly of her only family? It was beyond insulting. But then, he was a pirate after all. A man used to using any underhanded tactic in getting his own way.

"So a life of luxury and leisure is more important than honor? Am I correct in assuming that? I cannot say I'm not disappointed in you, my dear. I didn't think you were materialistic. I suppose I'm not such a good judge of character." Stephen did not follow her, and yet his words hit her like a whip.

Turning to face him she started at the anger she read in his gaze. "I hardly think you're a beacon on which others should strive for regarding good character and judgment." Disdain laced her tone. "You kidnapped me. Seduced me if you wish to throw stones at my head." Arabella hated that she was saying such things that were not the truth. The day she gave herself to Stephen, she did so willingly. "I never asked for this. I never asked to be taken away from the only life I knew. To be thrust on to the high seas with a pirate and his raggedy crew. And here you stand, upset and angry at me when I must refuse your charms, no matter how tempting, because I made a promise to someone else, long before I met you. You are being unfair," her voice broke and she fought to breathe.

"I'm being unfair?" He yelled, the men on the ship making themselves scarce. "I love you and you're choosing to walk away from that for the sake of your father's comfort, because let me assure you, *Miss Hester*, there will never be any love in your marriage. You will be used as a cover for Lord Montague's real desires and little else. I mourn the life you will lead. It will not be the one you've always wished for."

Arabella threw her belongings onto Lord Montague's ship. Her hands shook and she fisted them at her sides to stop the trembling. How she wanted to run to him, to say yes to all that he offered and let her father, her betrothed sort out their own mess. "Goodbye and good luck Captain Blackmore. I wish you well."

He bestowed a sweeping bow. "I don't need any luck, Miss Hester. You keep it. I feel you'll need it a lot more than I."

Arabella's father laughed. "You can try and run but the authorities will catch up with you to seek my revenge. Perhaps I may visit you in Newgate."

"There will be no authorities or further discussion involving them in relation to the captain." She turned and met her father's startled eye. "Push the subject and I will not marry Lord Montague under any circumstance. Do you understand, Father?"

He nodded, helped her board the other ship and pulled her toward the stairs to go below deck. At the threshold, Arabella turned to see a quick exchange between Lord Montague and Stephen. Her stomach rolled with nerves at having to leave the man she loved. Of course she'd always known the time would come when she would go, but it didn't make that time any easier when it arrived.

Her father of course wished for his daughter's happiness, no matter the circumstances or cost to the family. He'd brought her up to think this way, but it would seem when the time came for such choices, men were want to change their minds.

Stephen did not look her way again, and she bit back the tears that threatened. This would be the last time she'd ever see him. In her mind 's eye, she captured an image of him, every curve, every nuance of his being before he shouted out commands to set sail before disappearing below decks. Out of sight and out of her life. Forever.

CHAPTER 9

Arabella looked down at her simple blue morning gown and wiped away tears that refused to stop. The past four weeks without Stephen, without waking up next to him, talking to him, laughing with him had been the worst of her life.

She'd made a mistake and now it was too late to change her mind.

"The carriage is here, Arabella. We must leave," her father said, cold and autocratic as it had been from the moment they stepped foot in London. Not that she cared any longer. One could not care when one no longer had a heart that beat.

She stood and followed her father downstairs and toward the front door. Their two newly hired footmen bowed as she went past and she cringed at the extravagant lifestyle her father had started to live since her betrothal to Lord Montague was secured.

Stephen had been right all along. Her father had a problem handling money, and if his expenditures over the past few weeks were any indication it wouldn't take him very long to go through what blunt Lord Montague had as well.

She could almost feel sorry for her future husband... should he ever bother to visit her, that was. Not once since she'd been thrust into a carriage on the docks had he come to see her. Yes, missives were sent, notifying her of what he expected her to wear on their wedding day. The rules she should follow once his bride. The most glaringly obvious one being she was not to ask for consummation of the marriage until he was ready. Not that she wanted to sleep with the prig in any case. Even the thought of kissing the man after their wedding sent revulsion to her core.

And yet she wondered at his lordships decree that he would not sleep with her. What gentleman wasn't ready to claim his wife? None of it made any sense and Stephen's cryptic words flittered through her mind. What was it that she wasn't seeing.

She climbed into the carriage and settled back into the leather squabs as her father fussed with his cravat. "Not long now, my dear. I'm so pleased I'll be able to call you Lady Montague. It has a certain ring about it, don't you think?"

A terrible one perhaps... "Yes, Father, it's most exciting." Her voice dripped with boredom, something she had an inkling her life was going to be from now on. So different to what her life with Stephen might have been. Where was he right at this moment? Was he happy, sad, a thousand miles away on a distant ocean...?

The ride to St James was quick and before long Arabella made her way toward the large double wooden doors. Music started to play as she entered, her hand nestled softly over her father's. It would be a perfect day, a perfect wedding should she be marrying the man she loved.

But she was not. What a fool she'd been to think putting someone else's wants and desires above her own heart. Lord Montague didn't care for her and never would and she was being sold to the highest bidder, and all to keep her father accustomed to a lifestyle he could no longer afford.

Lord Montague looked stunning in his cream satin knee-breeches, perfectly cut blue coat and buckled shoes. He didn't bother to turn and watch her walk toward him. Instead his back was severely straight, rigid to the point of looking painful.

Her father gave her over to his lordship and returned to the pew. Arabella nodded to the priest for him to begin. She wouldn't look at Lord Montague. How could she? They were not a good match and nor did she desire him to be her husband. A role she loathed to think on and did not want. If she were truthful with herself, probably never wanted. Back in Malta when he had asked for her hand, she'd been so overjoyed a lord had asked to marry her, she had forgotten to ask herself if she cared that he did. Her father was certainly pleased, which made her also, but thinking back Arabella realized she didn't care at all for his lordship. Nor ever would.

They started to take their vows, repeating what the priest said to them. Compelled to look at his lordship, she was surprised to see the ashen and fear in Lord Montague's eyes as if he too was having second thoughts. Hope bloomed in her heart. Maybe there was a chance for all to see sense before it was too late.

She squeezed his hand. "Are you well, my lord?"

His attention wavered from her to her father's, the fear in his eyes increasing. "Of course, my dear. Just nervous, I believe."

The priest coughed and she glared at the man of the cloth who rolled his eyes.

Arabella shook her head. "No, it's not just nerves. You do not want to marry me any more than I wish to marry you." She turned to her father, done with all the secrets, and pretending all of this was acceptable. "What is going on here that I don't know about?"

"What do you mean? Proceed this instant. You're embarrassing the family."

She scoffed. "How can I embarrass anyone? There isn't anybody here to see." She turned back to his lordship. "Do you want to marry me, Frederick? And I want the truth."

His shoulders slumped, and he shook his head. "I do not." He took her hand. "There is something your father knows about me that he's blackmailing me with," he said, whispering the words so her father would not hear. "My lifestyle has never involved plans of marriage, but when one isn't careful enough, one can find oneself before a priest marrying a woman, no matter how lovely, that is not who he loves."

Realization struck her like a blow. How could she not have seen it? She nodded, understanding dawning on her over what Stephen was trying to warn her of all those weeks ago. "I will not marry you, my lord. Not today or ever." She smiled, hugging his lordship for the first time since their betrothal. "Whatever my father has threatened you with you must forget. I will not allow you to be a part of his deviant money-making schemes."

"What the hell do you think you're doing, child!" Her father scrambled toward them and clasped her arm. She bit back a whimper as his hold increased with every word. "I will ruin him should you not do as you're told. We'll be finished should you refuse to marry this man. Do you know what that means?"

Arabella wrenched her arm free, seeing her father clearly for the first time. A swindler, a pirate far worse than Stephen ever could be. "Of course I do, but I also know it's time you held yourself accountable for the way you live your life. Lord Montague should not be your bank just because you assume to know something of his life."

Her father's face mottled in anger, his skin turning as red as a lobster. "I forbid you to leave this church unmarried. I'm your father, the head of our household. You will do as you're told." His words thundered through the church and out the corner of her eye Arabella noted the priest jumped.

"I will not." Arabella stood nose to nose with him and refused to give in to her churning stomach. She'd never stood up for herself in such a way in her life. And although liberating, it was also terrifying. She supposed all her weeks with Stephen had given her the strength of mind to call out a wrong when she saw one. Not to sit idly by and allow bad things to happen, but to change them, make situations better if possible. "You cannot make me do something I disagree with. Not to mention threatening Lord Montague as well. How could you act so low? You're behaving in a way I'm unfamiliar with. Where is the loving, caring father that I know?"

"Finished, that's where," he shouted before his eyes widened in shock.

Arabella clasped her father's arm as he swayed. His knees buckled under his weight and she screamed for Lord

Montague's help as her father crumbled to the cold, tiled floor.

Commotion erupted behind her, the priest yelling for the altar boys to run for help. Arabella patted his cheek, trying to rouse him in any way she could. "Father? Wake up. Are you all right? Please talk to me."

He moaned but reached out to take her hand. "My chest. Pain," he mumbled, closing his eyes again.

Lord Montague placed his coat beneath her father's head. Arabella didn't know what to do or how to help him. She called out for water, but her parent just pushed it away when she went to help him drink.

"Please, Father. What can I do? What's happening?" She sniffed, the thought that he was dying before her eyes more than she could bear. He couldn't leave her after such a fight. For all his trouble making, his wayward lifestyle, he was her papa. She loved him. "What can we do?"

He shook his head, clasping his chest. "I'm sorry Arabella."

She kissed his cheek and hugged him. "I'm sorry too. I love you. Please don't leave me." Arabella sobbed as the last beat of her father's heart thumped beneath her ear, before silence reigned. She lay there, the thought that she'd lost the last member of her family and in such a way, under such terrible circumstances beyond comprehension.

Lord Montague pulled her away and gave comfort as best he could. "It'll be all right, Arabella. I'll ensure you will be fully taken care of."

She sobbed against his chest. Even after all her father had put this man through he'd still ensure her well-being. Perhaps her opinion of his lordship was wrong. "No. You don't have to. This is not your responsibility. You've been too kind after everything I've put you through. How will I ever thank you?"

He pulled out a handkerchief and wiped her tears. "No thanks are needed." A group of men, one carrying a bag and Arabella assumed to be a doctor, ran into the church. She sat on a pew knowing there wasn't anything they could do for her father.

Guilt over their fight, one of the last moments she had with the man who raised her tore at her soul. How could she be so heartless?

"I will not let you think this is your fault." Lord Montague sat beside her. "The doctor is saying it looks like he's had a heart seizure of some kind. I can see by your face you're blaming yourself and you should not. Terrible tragedies happen, my dear. No one is to blame."

"But I fought with him, made his temper rise more than I should."

"And rightly so. What your father was doing was wrong and you're a remarkable woman having stood up for me and your life like you did." His lordship took her hand, patting it kindly. "Do not forget he apologized, Arabella. He knew within himself that what he was doing was wrong. Please do not blame yourself about what has transpired here today. It could've happened anywhere and at any time."

The doctor echoed Lord Montague's words, but it still didn't make the passing of her only living parent easier. From this moment on, she was truly alone. Even Stephen was lost to her and his lordship would no doubt go on with his life less a wife just as he should.

What would she do? Where would she go? Once her father's debts were settled by the sale of their London home, she'd be homeless, friendless even. To cry off a marriage to a peer of the realm was no small thing. From this day forward, she would truly be ruined.

Tears streamed down her cheeks. Sure, she had wished for freedom to choose her own future, to pick her own husband and the sort of life she wanted to lead, but never at the cost of her father's life.

Never that.

CHAPTER 10

Stephen strolled across a paddock covered with heather and wildflowers which would, over the next few weeks, give way to a highland winter. And if the chilling wind from the north was any indication, this year may the coldest he'd had to live through in many years.

Sailing and living mostly in foreign places with sandy beaches and a warm sun on his back was a pleasant distant memory that haunted him. Well, it would haunt him until his body acclimatized to Scotland. He'd never known such a cold place and yet he would not wish to be anywhere else in the world.

In the distance rose the small castle he now called home. The brown and gold stone a beacon in the otherwise green landscape. It was all he had now. Having sold his ship to give his men the future they deserved, the funds that were left over were soon eaten up with the repairs he'd had to make to the leaking castle roof.

The home farms should start to make profit again and even though there wasn't a lot of blunt left from his smuggling days, it was enough to keep him and his mother, who'd he'd moved up here as well, reasonably comfortable for a year or two until the estate was self-sufficient once more.

A distant rumble sounded in the south and he turned to peer at the only road that ran into his property. He frowned having not expected anyone of than the Duke of Dale, who wasn't due to arrive for some weeks.

A carriage, covered with dust and mud from the unforgiving Scottish highland roads materialized after coming around the last curve in the road. The cattle looked well defined and expensive. Maybe Gabe had come early.

He made his way toward the house by following an old sheep track that wound its way down the hillside. The staff came out to greet the vehicle and to help the occupants to step down.

Stephen's step faltered when a vision in an emerald green traveling gown alighted and looked about with interest. Instead of her long brown locks falling loose about her shoulders, they were coiled up into a coiffure on top of her head.

He continued walking on, watching her, taking his fill of the one woman he'd longed to see more than the highlands sunrise.

Arabella…

She followed his footman into the house and he lost sight of her. Stephen went around the back of the house, dropped the game birds he'd been able to kill in to the kitchens, and notified cook that he'd have a guest at dinner.

The jovial woman took the news with aplomb and busied herself with renewed vigor having someone other than his mother and himself to cook for.

Stephen headed for the front drawing room, once the castle's old solar and entered without knocking. Arabella stood beside the bookcase that covered one whole wall, her attention riveted on the works of the greats. "Good afternoon, Lady Montague. I had not expected to see you again." He shut the door, seating himself at the desk while trying to busy himself with the mail with little success. The thought she was here, married and no longer accessible to him drove him insane.

It was not to be borne. He closed his eyes for a moment, and fought for calm lest he throw his blotter against the wall or something even more ridiculous.

"Hello, Stephen." She sat in the chair before his desk and smiled. "I'm sorry to intrude on you without notice, but I was afraid you wouldn't see me if I wrote and notified you of my intention to call."

"And what possibly could be your intention? I believe everything we've said to one another has left no stone unturned." She paled a little at his words and he wanted to go to her, to hold her, comfort her in any way he could. Stephen gritted his teeth and didn't move.

"You never told me about your lineage or about this ancestral home you've purchased since your grandfather lost it all at a game of cards."

Stephen started. Not many knew that's why. "I see you've been talking to the Duke of Dale."

She gave a decisive nod. "I have. And what a tale of woe he told me." A small frown line appeared between her perfect brows. "Why did you never tell me?"

Just the thought of how low the family had fallen left him hollow inside. "No one knows, and I don't like talking about my family or their fall from grace. Life on the sea was the only option left for me and I made the most of it. I may no longer have a title, but I have my ancestral home back. I'm satisfied."

"For what it's worth, I'm proud of your accomplishments. You have not had the easiest life, and yet you still achieved your goals. I too can only wish that should my situation ever be similar that I would act the same. Not settle for less than what I deserve."

A lump formed in Stephen's throat having not expected to hear such pride in her words. Nor that Arabella's belief in him was so important. Yet, it was.

"Are you angry I came? I thought…" her voice trailed off and she fidgeted with the hem of her glove.

"What, Miss Hester?"

Arabella stood and went to the sideboard and after pouring herself a brandy, downed it in one swallow. She coughed before walking over to him, rolling back his chair and sitting before him on his desk.

Stephen's body thrummed in anticipation. There was never any doubt Arabella could be a seductive minx when she wished, but he never thought she'd be so once married. Had she married him at least he'd never allow her out of his sight. Lord Montague was a fool who didn't know a gem when he held one in his hand. "What are you doing?" He cleared his throat, his voice sounding even tight to his own ears.

"I want you. All of you." She sat on his lap and pushed a lock of hair out of his eyes. "I never married Lord Montague. You are the man I want to marry and to spend the rest of my days with. It is you I love." Stephen watched her a moment, read the sincerity in her gaze. *She never married Lord Montague?*

He pulled back, startled by her words. "What happened?" Sadness clouded her eyes and he frowned. "Tell me what happened, Arabella."

She sighed. "The wedding went ahead as planned. I

would do my duty for my father, but as I was walking down the aisle, no guests present to celebrate our wedding and my betrothed who looked like I was a noose about his neck I realized I couldn't do it. I couldn't put another person's happiness before my own. I was tired of being ordered about by the men in my life." She gave him a small smile. "I halted the ceremony and discussed my fears with Lord Montague. He was in agreement. It seems Father had been blackmailing him in relation to sexual trysts with men. I was horrified to find out Father had acted so low." She paused, her lip wobbling. "My father passed away."

Stephen swore, not believing what he was hearing. "Your father died! How?"

"He collapsed in the church, before Lord Montague and me. There was nothing we could do. A doctor said it was a heart seizure or possibly a problem within his brain." A tear slid down her cheek and Stephen wrenched her into his arms, trying to comfort her in any way he could.

How had he not heard of this? "Why did you not write? I would've come for you."

"I had to sell the London house as Father had placed it in my name to keep it from the debt collectors. There was so much to be done. The funeral, chasing down vowels and paying them in full. You were so right about what my father had been up to. I apologize for calling you a lying cad. You are not one." She nuzzled against his neck and he held her tighter, never wishing her to be parted from him again.

He smiled and kissed her, lingered as her sweetness burst through his soul like light. "I'm a cad, there is no doubt, but I'll never lie to you. I also want you to know these past weeks without you have been hellish. The thought of you belonging to another, and someone who would never treat you with reverence as I would drove me insane." He paused, catching her attention. "I never kept the payment from your father."

She started, her eyes wide with shock. "You didn't?"

"I did not," he said, shaking his head. "I sent it all back, every penny. You are worth more to me than any blunt that was owed, and the thought of taking payment in lieu of having you made me ill." He wiped a tear from her cheek. "I love you Arabella."

She hugged him about his neck and he could hear her smile in her words. "You love me? Is that all?"

"Greedy minx." He raised his brow. "What else would you like for me to say? Maybe…" he paused, grinning. "Will you marry me?" A light blush stole over her cheeks and Stephen had never seen anyone more beautiful.

"Yes. I will marry you, my gentleman pirate. And I will love you forever."

Stephen kissed her hard, reveled in the feel of her body against his chest, the only woman he ever wanted to feel again. He stood and lifted her onto the desk, quickly hiking up her traveling gown skirts. He had to have her. Here. Now. Later he would lay her down on his bed, pay homage to her delectable body, but right now, after weeks apart, his desire was too great.

She ripped at his frontfalls and Stephen gritted his teeth as her touch swept over his engorged cock. Damn it. He was so hard for her it hurt. He thrust into her waiting palm when she freed him and it was heaven on earth.

Cool air kissed his buttocks as his breeches fell to the floor. Stephen nibbled her chin as he slid her toward the edge of the desk. She laughed and wrapped her legs about his waist. "Damn, I want you. I don't know how gentle I'll be."

She clasped his back, her nails scoring his skin as she held him close. "I don't care. Do as you will."

Stephen positioned himself at her core, her heat, her readiness for him beyond his imaginings. What a marvelous woman and now she was his. Possession took hold and he slid easily and fully into her. Her body clasped him tight, drawing him toward a blissful end that he was determined she too would reach. Today was just the beginning of many tomorrows.

How lucky he was.

* * *

Arabella moaned as Stephen finally claimed her. Their time a part felt like years. Had it really only been weeks? He thrust into her, his body a perfect fit. God she had missed him. Had missed the adventure he had wrapped around his soul.

And his love making was no different. Hot, hard and fulfilling seemed to be the man's motto. How lucky was she to have been kidnapped by him.

She played with his buttocks and forced him to take her just as she liked. Stephen's bed sport had always been exciting, but today it was different. There was an edge of possession mixed with desperation. A desperation born out of love and the thought that what one had and adored would never be theirs again. Arabella knew the emotion well, having lived the hell during their weeks apart. "Yes," she gasped as with each stroke he pushed her toward a pinnacle she longed to reach. He clasped her leg and changed the pace of their lovemaking, going slower but deeper each time.

Arabella threw her head back, her body coiling tight

with impending release. There was something arousing being dressed but taken in full daylight and on a desk. Memories of such an escapade on Stephen's ship slipped through her mind and she smiled. What a fabulous life she was about to begin.

"Come for me, darling." He continued to take her, his strong, capable hands biting in to her buttocks. "Let me feel you shatter around me."

His dirty talk inflamed her more. She held onto him, urged him to take her harder, faster. He did and within moments, the sensation of absolute bliss thrummed throughout her body. Arabella screamed his name, pulled him to her until he too exclaimed an echoing release.

They collapsed on his desk, both breathing hard as if they had run a thousand miles. Arabella smiled. "I'm going to enjoy being your wife. I think I will enjoy it very much." She met his gaze and read amusement in his blue eyes.

"That's just as it should be. I wouldn't have anything less for my bonny English lass," he said, teasing her with his Scottish brogue.

"And that's exactly why I'm yours. Forever."

He nodded, his face becoming serious. "Yes. Forever, and then some."

Dear Reader,

Thank you for taking the time to read *High Seas & High Stakes Series Bundle.* I hope you enjoyed His Lady Smuggler and Her Gentleman Pirate.

I adore my readers, and I'm so thankful for your support. If you're able, I would appreciate an honest review of *High Seas & High Stakes Bundle.* As they say, feed an author, leave a review! Alternatively, you can keep in contact with me by visiting my website or following me online. You can contact me at www.tamaragill.com or email me at tamaragillauthor@gmail.com.

If you'd like to learn about, Tempt Me, Your Grace, book one in my League of Unweddable Gentlemen series, please read on. I have included the prologue for your reading pleasure.

Tamara Gill

TEMPT ME, YOUR GRACE

LEAGUE OF UNWEDDABLE
GENTLEMEN, BOOK 1

*She was banished from England…and she banished him from her
heart.*

*Upon her return to England following her father's death, Miss Ava
Knight becomes the owner of one of the largest racehorse estates in the
country. There's only one problem: the future of the estate requires a*

strong breeding program with the services of a stallion named, Titan. A shame that the horse is owned by a man she swore to never see again.

The Duke of Whitstone, Tate Wells, was heartbroken when Ava abandoned him on the night of their elopement, and he vowed to never lay eyes on Ava again. Despite Tate's unwillingness to forgive Ava, she comes to his aid during a deliberately lit fire at his estate. Someone is determined to destroy them. Now, the two are forced to work together to ensure the safety of their horses and their homes.

Will their previous feelings for each other rekindle their love, or will their feelings stall out at the starting gates?

PROLOGUE

Knight Stables, Berkshire, 1816

Miss Avelina Knight, Ava to those close to her, tightened the girth of her mount, and checked that the saddle wouldn't slip whilst hoisting herself onto one stirrup. With a single candle burning in the sconce on the stables' wall, she worked as quickly and as noiselessly as she could in the hopes that the stable hands that slept in the lofts above wouldn't wake.

Pleased that the saddle would hold, and that her mount was well watered before her departure, she walked Manny out of the stables as silently as possible, cringing when the horse's shod feet made a clip clop sound with each step.

Ava blew out the candle as she walked past it, and picking up her small bag, threw it over her horse's neck before hoisting herself up into the saddle. She sat there a minute, listening for any noise, or the possibility that someone was watching. Happy that everything remained quiet, she nudged her mount and started for the eastern gate.

There was still time and she didn't need to rush, now that she was on her way. Tate had said he'd meet her at their favorite tree at three in the morning, and it was only half past two.

She pushed Manny into a canter, winding her way through several horse yards that surrounded her home and past the gallop her father used to train their racing stock. Or what was once her home. From tonight onward, her life would finally begin. With Tate, she would travel the world, make love under the stars if they so wished, and not have to be slaves to either of their families' whims or Society and its strictures.

Tate and she would find a new life. A new beginning. Just the two of them until they expanded their family to add children in a few years.

Pleasure warmed her heart at the knowledge, and she couldn't stop the soft laugh of delight which escaped her.

In time, Ava hoped her father would forgive her, and maybe when they returned, happily married with children even, her father would be pleased.

The shadowy figure of a man stood beneath the tree. Yet from the stance and girth of the gentleman, it did not look like Tate. Coldness swept over her skin, and she narrowed her eyes, trying to make out who was waiting for her. Her stomach in knots, she pushed her horse forward unsure what this new development meant.

Ava looked about, but could see no one else. With a couple of more steps she gasped when she finally made out the ghostly form. Her father.

Her heart pounded a frantic beat. How was it he was here and not Tate? They had been so careful, so discreet. Why, they had not even circulated within the same social sphere to be heard whispering or planning. With Tate being the heir to his father, the Duke of Whitstone and Ava only the daughter of a racehorse notable, their lives couldn't be more different.

Ava rode her horse up to the tree. She saw little point in turning back.

Pulling up before her father, she met his gaze, as much of it as she could make out under the moonlit night.

"Ava, climb down, I wish to speak to you."

His tone was not angry, but guarded, and the pit of her stomach lurched at the notion that something dreadful had happened to Tate. Had he been hurt? Why wasn't he here to meet her instead?

She jumped down, walking up to him, her mount following on her heels.

"Papa, what are you doing here?" she asked, needing to know and knowing there was little point in ignoring the fact that he'd found her out.

She dropped her horse's reins, and her mount reached down to nibble on the grass.

Her father's face took on a stern cast. "The Marquess of Cleremore will not be meeting you here, Ava. I received a note late last night notifying me that, as we speak, his lordship has been sent to London to catch the first boat out to New York. From what his father, the Duke of Whitstone, states, this was the marquess' decision. Tate confided in his father the predicament he'd found himself in with you, and that he didn't know how to untangle himself from having to marry a woman who was not his equal."

Ava stared at her father, unable to fathom what he was saying. Hollowness opened up in her chest and she clasped her shawl as if to halt its progress. Tate had left her? No, it couldn't be true. "But that doesn't make any sense, Papa. Tate loves me. He said so himself at this very spot." Surely she couldn't have been wrong about his affections. People did not declare such emotions unless they were true. She certainly had not.

She loved Tate. Ava thought back to all the times he'd taken liberties with her, kissing her, touching her, spending copious amounts of time with her and it had all been meaningless to him. She had been a mere distraction, a plaything for a man of his stature.

Her stomach roiled at the idea and she stumbled to the tree, clutching it for support. "No. I do not believe it. Tate wouldn't do that to me. He loves me as I love him and we're going to marry each other." Ava stared down at the ground for a moment, her mind reeling before she rounded on her father. "I need to see him. He needs to tell me this to my face."

"Lord Cleremore has already left for town. And by morning, he'll be on a ship to America." Her father sighed, coming over to her and taking her hand. "I thought your attachment to him was a passing folly. His lordship was never for you, my dear. We train and breed racehorses and, in England, people like us do not marry future dukes."

Ava stared at her father, not believing this was happening. She'd thought tonight would be the start of forever, but it was now the beginning of the end. Her eyes smarted and she was powerless to hold onto her composure. "But I love him," she whispered, her voice cracking.

Her father, a proud but humble man from even humbler beginnings, straightened his spine. "I know you think you did, but it wasn't love. You're young, too young to be throwing your life away on a boy who would have his way with you and then marry another titled, well-connected woman."

"I'm not ruined or touched, father. Please don't speak

in such a way." She didn't want to imagine that Tate could treat her with so little respect, but what her father said was worth thinking over. The past few weeks with Tate had left very little room other than to plan, to plot. Would they have thought differently, would Tate have acted differently if he'd been older, more mature? If his departure showed anything, it was certainly that what her father was saying was true. He had regretted his choice and had left instead of facing her. Letting her down as a gentleman should, had not been his course. It showed how little he thought of her and the love she'd so ardently declared to him.

She swiped at her cheeks, wanting to scream into the night at the unfairness of it all.

"I'm sorry," she said, looking at her half boots and not able to meet his gaze. *How could he have done this to me?* She would never forgive him.

He sighed. "There is one more thing, my dear."

More! What else could there possibly be to say! "What, papa?" she asked, dread formed like a knot in her stomach at her father's ashen countenance. She'd seen a similar look from him when he'd come to tell her of her mother's passing and it was a visage she'd never wanted to see again. Ava clutched the tree harder.

"I'm sending you away to finishing school in France. I've enrolled you at Madame. Dufour's Refining School for Girls. It's located in southern France. It comes highly recommended and will help prepare you for what's to come in your life; namely, running Knight Stables, taking over from me when the time comes."

Finishing school! "You're sending me to France! But Papa, I don't need finishing school. You know that I'm more than capable of taking over the running of the stables already. And I know my manners, how to act in both upper- and lower-class society. Please do not send me away. I won't survive without you and our horses. Don't take that away from me, too." *Not when I've already lost the happiness of which I was so certain.*

He shushed her, pulling her into his arms. Ava shoved him away, pacing before him.

Her father held out his hand, trying to pacify her. "You'll thank me one day. Trust me when I tell you, this is a good thing for you, and I'll not be moved on my decision. We're leaving for Dover tomorrow and I, myself, will accompany you to ensure your safe arrival."

"What." She stopped pacing. "Father, please don't do this. I promise not to do such a silly, foolish thing again. You said yourself Tate was leaving. There is no reason to send me away as well." Just saying such a thing aloud hurt and Ava clutched her stomach. To have loved and lost Tate would be hard enough; nevertheless being sent away to a foreign country, alone and without any friends or support was too much to bear.

He came over to her, pulling her against him and kissing her hair. "This is a good opportunity for you, Ava. I have worked hard, saved, and invested to enable me to give you all that a titled child could receive. I want this for you. Lord Cleremore may not think that you're suitable for him, but we shall prove him wrong. Make me proud, use the education to better yourself, and come home. Promise me you will do so."

Ava slumped against him. Her father had never been flexible on things and once he'd made a decision it was final. There was no choice; she would have to do as he said. "I will go as I see there is little I can say to change your mind."

"That's my girl." He pulled back and whistled for her mount.

She couldn't even manage a half-smile as Manny trotted over to them.

"Let us go. I'm sure by the time we arrive back home breakfast will not be far away."

Using a nearby log, Ava hoisted herself up onto the saddle. The horse, as if knowing her way home, started ambling down the hill. Light shone in the eastern sky and glancing to her left, Ava watched the sun rise over her land. Observed the dawn of a new day, marking a new future even for her, one that did not include Tate, Marquess Cleremore and future Duke of Whitstone.

A lone tear slid down her cheek and she promised herself, there and then, never to cry over Tate again or any other man. She'd given him her heart and trust and he had callously broken them. That the tear drying on her cheek would be the last she ever afforded him.

And his precious dukedom that he loved so dearly. More dearly than her.

Want to read more? Tempt Me, Your Grace available now!

WAYWARD WOODVILLES
COMING SOON!

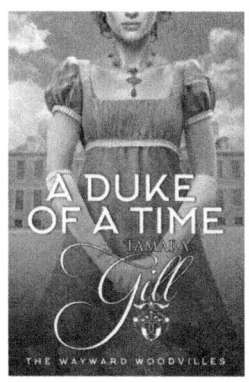

New spicy Regency romance series
Coming February 2022!
Pre-order your copy today!

SERIES BY TAMARA GILL

The Wayward Woodvilles

Royal House of Atharia

League of Unweddable Gentlemen

Kiss the Wallflower

Lords of London

To Marry a Rogue

A Time Traveler's Highland Love

A Stolen Season

Scandalous London

High Seas & High Stakes

Daughters Of The Gods

Stand Alone Books

Defiant Surrender

To Sin with Scandal

Outlaws

ABOUT THE AUTHOR

Tamara is an Australian author who grew up in an old mining town in country South Australia, where her love of history was founded. So much so, she made her darling husband travel to the UK for their honeymoon, where she dragged him from one historical monument and castle to another.

A mother of three, her two little gentlemen in the making, a future lady (she hopes) and a part-time job keep her busy in the real world, but whenever she gets a moment's peace she loves to write romance novels in an array of genres, including regency, medieval and time travel.

www.tamaragill.com
tamaragillauthor@gmail.com

Made in the USA
Middletown, DE
24 February 2023

25550579R00126